He opened the d⬛⬛⬛⬛⬛⬛⬛⬛⬛⬛⬛⬛k and waited.

Nothing.

Still, Luna's low grow⬛⬛⬛⬛⬛⬛⬛⬛⬛ slid out through the opening and ran in a crouch to the edge of the vehicle.

A blur of motion caught the corner of his eye. He called out, "Police," then fired in the general direction.

He opened the back door of the SUV and the rear hatch for Luna, and then ran around to the driver's side. Luna gracefully jumped into the rear.

In mere seconds they were barreling down the rutted driveway, leaving the cabin in the dust.

Just when he thought they were in the clear, he heard the crack of a rifle.

ALASKA K-9 UNIT

*These state troopers fight for justice
with the help of their brave canine partners.*

Laura Scott has always loved romance and read faith-based books by Grace Livingston Hill in her teenage years. She's thrilled to have been given the opportunity to retire from thirty-eight years of nursing to become a full-time author. Laura has published over thirty books for Love Inspired Suspense. She has two adult children and lives in Milwaukee, Wisconsin, with her husband of thirty-five years. Please visit Laura at laurascottbooks.com, as she loves to hear from her readers.

Books by Laura Scott

Love Inspired Suspense

Alaska K-9 Unit

Tracking Stolen Secrets

Justice Seekers

Soldier's Christmas Secrets
Guarded by the Soldier
Wyoming Mountain Escape

Callahan Confidential

Shielding His Christmas Witness
The Only Witness
Christmas Amnesia
Shattered Lullaby
Primary Suspect
Protecting His Secret Son

Visit the Author Profile page at Harlequin.com for more titles.

TRACKING STOLEN SECRETS

LAURA SCOTT

LOVE INSPIRED SUSPENSE
INSPIRATIONAL ROMANCE

Special thanks and acknowledgment are given to Laura Scott for her contribution to the Alaska K-9 Unit miniseries.

LOVE INSPIRED SUSPENSE
INSPIRATIONAL ROMANCE

Recycling programs
for this product may
not exist in your area.

ISBN-13: 978-1-335-72251-5

Tracking Stolen Secrets

Copyright © 2021 by Harlequin Books S.A.

This edition published by arrangement with Harlequin Books S.A.

For questions and comments about the quality of this book, please contact us at CustomerService@Harlequin.com.

Love Inspired
22 Adelaide St. West, 40th Floor
Toronto, Ontario M5H 4E3, Canada
www.Harlequin.com

Printed in U.S.A.

My soul melteth for heaviness:
strengthen thou me according unto thy word.
—*Psalm* 119:28

This book is dedicated to Lisa Iding, sister of my heart. Stay courageous and strong through your cancer journey and know God is with you, always.

ONE

Alaska K-9 State Trooper Helena Maddox headed up the grassy embankment within Denali National park, looking for any sign indicating her estranged twin, Zoe, had been in the area recently. Upon reaching the crest, she knelt beside her K-9, Luna, a Norwegian elkhound. She ran her fingers through the animal's fluffy silver-gray fur before opening the evidence bag and offering it to her partner.

"This is Zoe. Seek Zoe. Seek!"

Luna buried her dark face in the bag, taking in the scent of a scarf Zoe had left behind well over a year ago, then lifted her nose to the air, sniffing as the gentle July breeze washed over them.

"Seek Zoe." She repeated as she released the K-9 from her leash, giving her room to roam.

Gazing upward, Helena caught a glimpse of the tallest peak in America. Denali never failed to steal her breath. Today she couldn't see as much of the mountain as she would have liked, thanks to the low clouds hinting at an upcoming storm. But this wasn't a leisurely visit. She'd driven straight from Anchorage after receiving the uncharacteristic call from her fraternal twin sister.

Helena? I'm in big trouble— The connection had abruptly ended, and each time Helena had tried to call the number back, the phone went straight to voice mail. Zoe's full mailbox was not accepting messages.

Helena wasn't necessarily surprised at Zoe being in trouble. Her sister had skated by in life, using her looks to get what she wanted. Zoe was attracted to bad boys, regardless of how they tended to ride along the edge of the law. But lately things had gotten worse. Not hearing from her in over a year, despite Helena's many attempts at reaching out, had been bad, but receiving Zoe's distress call had spurred a dire sense of urgency.

"Where are you, Zoe?" She looked around the rather desolate area. Denali Park had hundreds of thousands of acres of wilderness. The Alaska K-9 Unit, headquartered in Anchorage, consisted of several team members, each with their own area of expertise. Their leader, Colonel Lorenza Gallo, had created the unit ten years ago to supplement law enforcement across the state, especially in rural areas that couldn't afford their own K-9 program. Eli Partridge, the team's tech guru, had provided this general area as the location from where Zoe's cell call had originated. But the land was vast and wide, covering an extensive range of possible hiding spots.

And it wasn't like Zoe to rough it. Her sister had always preferred the finer things in life.

In the valley below, Helena could see a handful of hotels located at the base of the mountain. A brand-new, much larger hotel was also visible. It was located several miles away from the others, giving it a sense of exclusivity.

Why would Zoe be out here? Was she working at one of the hotels? That made more sense than the thought of her communing with nature.

The radio clipped to her collar crackled and she reached up to respond. "Will? Did you find anything related to Zoe or the burglaries?"

"Maybe." Will Stryker and his K-9 Scout, a black-and-white border collie with a nose for narcotics, had gone in the opposite direction. "I see what looks like a cave. Scout and I are going to check it out."

"Copy that." She released the radio and glanced around again, searching for Luna. The dog's zigzag pattern indicated she was still searching for Zoe's scent, her hunt drawing her several yards away.

Helena was headed toward Luna when the sharp crack of a rifle rang out. At that exact moment, she was hit hard from behind and sent face-first to the ground in a bone-jarring thud.

"Oomph." The momentum carried her and the person who'd hit her forward so they rolled down the side of the hill.

What in the world?

"Are you okay?" a deep male voice asked.

A nice attacker? Helena lifted her head in time to see Luna wheel around toward her, low growls reverberating from the K-9's throat.

"Were you hit?" The massive weight on top of her shifted, allowing her to breathe. "Are you bleeding?"

"Not—hit," she wheezed. The voice sounded familiar and when she realized who the man was, she quickly lifted a hand to her K-9 partner. "Stop, Luna! Heel!"

The dog halted just two feet away, but continued barking, making her displeasure known.

"What is that? Some kind of wolf?"

"She's a Norwegian elkhound." Helena pushed herself up, glancing around to look at the brown hired muscular guy who'd tackled her. "Everett Brand."

His dark brown gaze narrowed. "Helena

Maddox. You work for the Alaska K-9 Unit, right? We spoke on the phone just yesterday."

She nodded. By way of introduction, it wasn't much. Everett was a local cop from Anchorage. She'd seen him on occasion, but they hadn't really interacted much, until he'd called her yesterday to ask about Zoe.

Their conversation hadn't been cordial. He'd claimed her sister was a hard-core criminal while she'd instinctively defended her twin despite not having seen Zoe in a long time.

Now Everett Brand was here in Denali and in the same general location where her sister had been.

She eased upright, sitting on her knees. Now that the shock of being hit had faded, she realized the cop who was trying to arrest her sister had actually saved her life.

Helena released a quavering breath. She was grateful that he'd come to her rescue, even if his timing was a bit too coincidental for her peace of mind.

"Stay down," Everett warned. "I'm not sure which way the shot came from."

"Likely from the east." Obeying his command, she called Luna to her side. "The shooter will be well hidden in the mountains, and there's nowhere to hide beyond the road to the west." She lifted her hand to her radio. "Will?

Stay where you are," she told her colleague. "A shot has been fired. Repeat, shot fired and location of the shooter is unknown."

"Copy that, Helena. You okay?"

"Yes. I'll be in touch." She clicked off the radio.

Everett frowned, his dark brown gaze suspicious. "Will who?"

"Will Stryker and his border collie Scout are also members of our K-9 team. He's assisting me in the search." Helena was acutely aware of the intensity of Everett's dark eyes. She looked away, not liking the fact that they were still out in the open. The hill protected them somewhat if indeed the shooter was in the east, but not enough if the assailant managed to find higher ground. "We need to get to the vehicle and alert the park rangers about what happened."

"Yeah." Despite being a cop, Everett was dressed casually in cargo shorts, dark brown T-shirt and hiking boots. Too bad he was working against her, because he was a good looking man. "I'm sure the guy is long gone, or we'd be hearing more gunfire, but I like your idea of getting to the SUV."

Her white SUV with the yellow-and-blue state trooper logo wrapped along the side was parked in a lookout alcove off the main park road. Cars were only permitted on this road as far as Savage River, from that point forward only tour buses were allowed. She'd been granted special access because she was a member of the Alaska K-9 Unit.

"Okay, I'll go first. Come, Luna." She didn't wait for his response but sprang upright and ran for her SUV, Luna easily keeping pace beside her.

In seconds, she could feel Everett's towering presence behind her, his footsteps matching hers. He was so close that she could hear his breathing. What was he doing? She'd expected to use the SUV as a shield to provide cover for him, but apparently he was taking his role as her protector seriously.

As if she couldn't protect herself.

There was no additional gunfire as she reached her police SUV. Hunkering down behind the vehicle, she took in a deep breath and let it out slowly as Everett dropped down beside her.

"I think the shooter is gone," he said.

She glanced at him. "Why are you here? Are you following me?"

He scoffed. "Not hardly." He stared at her for a moment. "I have to say, I never realized how much you look like your sister."

"You think so?" She shook her head. "Zoe's hair is a bit lighter than mine. She's prettier and shorter than me by two inches. We're not identical twins."

"She must have dyed her hair then, because in the recent photo I have of her, she looks just like you." His gaze turned thoughtful. "I wonder if that's why the perp took that shot? From a distance, he may have thought you were Zoe, especially if he was only focused on your face."

Her heart thumped against her sternum as his words sank deep. Running from someone with a gun was trouble. Really bad trouble. A wave of helplessness washed over her. What on earth had Zoe gotten herself mixed up in?

Everett tore his gaze from Helena Maddox's clear green eyes with an effort.

Being this close, he could see the obvious differences between Helena and her twin. Zoe's picture, taken from a security camera in the early morning hours just a week ago, displayed a hard edge that he didn't see in this pretty state trooper. Zoe might be considered by some to be more beautiful, but he found light sprinkling of freckles across Helena's nose rather cute.

Oh, no. That's not right. He didn't notice women. He didn't call them cute or beautiful. He wasn't interested in dating or any of that relationship stuff.

Losing his wife and infant son three years ago had been the worst day of his life.

His fault. They were dead because of him. Because of a rookie mistake he'd made. Not that he'd been a rookie, which is why he should have known better.

Losing Sheila and Collin had left a gaping hole in his heart. One he had no intention of filling ever again.

"So, you never answered my question," Helena said, jarring him from his thoughts. "What are you doing all the way out here?"

"Hiking." It wasn't a lie. He had been hiking, while also searching for an indication of Zoe Maddox being nearby. "I'm staying here for a bit."

"In Denali?" Helena's bright green eyes rounded in surprise. The way she stroked her dog's fur, murmuring reassurances to the animal, almost made him want to smile. *Almost.* "How did you manage that? Reservations for any of the lodging sites here, including the campground, need to be made months in advance."

"I've had the same cabin rental reserved for the month of July for the past several years."

She frowned. "You're trying to tell me you're being here is just a big fat coincidence?"

He shrugged. "Believe what you want." He

wasn't about to get into the details around his personal life. Coming to the mountain cabin had been Sheila's idea initially, and after losing her and Collin, he'd continued the tradition in their absence.

Even though being here, relaxing in the mountains without his family, had been impossibly difficult. The gaping wound might have scabbed over, but the barest hint of a memory would bring waves upon waves of pain bubbling like lava through the crater of his heart.

Frankly, he was grateful for the distraction of following a lead that indicated Zoe was here in Denali. After failing to find her in Anchorage over the past two weeks, he hadn't delayed in making the four-plus-hour drive to Denali.

"I see." Helena's expression was still skeptical as she gave the dog one last pat. "Well, I need to talk to the park rangers. Not that there's much for them to do to help us track down the perp. We can walk the area, but finding a brass shell casing out here will be like searching for gold in the Savage River."

"I'll come with you." He glanced around and rose to his feet. "I know where the ranger station is located."

"I'm sure you do." She stood, her head barely reaching his chin. "Come, Luna."

He was impressed with how well the furry

beast listened to her. The animal wore a K-9 vest and seemed eager to please. Everett's experience with the K-9 cops was limited, but he'd liked seeing the variety of breeds they used. Helena rained attention on the animal then opened the back of the SUV. Without hesitation, the dog nimbly leaped inside.

"What were *you* doing out here?" he asked, eyeing the plastic bag containing what appeared to be a red scarf dangling from the utility belt of her uniform. Actually, now that he eyed her clothing, he wondered if his theory about the shooter mistaking her for Zoe was wrong. The state trooper uniform consisted of a light blue short-sleeved shirt paired with navy blue slacks. Helena wasn't wearing her trooper hat, though—he'd noticed it sitting on the passenger seat. "Are you on duty?"

"Yes." She didn't elaborate, which made him suspicious.

"You can't work cases in Denali without cooperation from the Park Service." He knew that because, to search for Zoe, he'd had to get special dispensation himself. The park rangers were busy in the short summer months of Alaska, so they hadn't argued when he'd presented his case, relieved to have his help.

"I'm aware. Trust me, the K-9 Unit works closely with all aspects of law enforcement."

She shut the hatch of the SUV and arched her brow. "Even local cops like you."

He felt the corner of his mouth twitch in what might have been a weak attempt at a smile. Climbing into the passenger seat, he moved her hat to the back and pulled on his seat belt.

The drive to the park rangers' headquarters didn't take long.

Everett followed Helena and Luna into the building, listening as she made her statement. He added the pertinent details from his end, and Ranger Arch Hanley took tons of notes.

"And you're sure you don't have any idea who may have done this?" Arch asked.

"No." Helena didn't look at him or offer the possibility of being mistaken for her twin as the reason she might be in danger.

"It's not often poachers shoot at state troopers," Arch pointed out. "Maybe it was an attempt to scare you off."

"Yeah, well that's not going to work. I need to continue canvassing the area." Helena thrust her chin forward, revealing a stubborn streak. "I only wanted you to be aware, in case anyone from your team stumbles across someone with a gun."

"Guns aren't allowed in the park outside of hunting season. You can be sure that anyone with a weapon will be questioned."

"What about those with concealed carry permits?" Everett asked.

Arch grimaced. "They're allowed in."

Great. That meant more folks than not likely had weapons. Maybe not a rifle, though, outside of hunting season, which is what he believed he'd heard. Especially since the shot had come from a distance.

Not that it mattered. In the end, there wasn't anything else for the ranger to do.

Helena appeared just as frustrated when they went back outside. "I don't like this. If the shooter took aim at me to get me away from the area, then I need to go back and continue searching."

He tensed. "I don't think that's a good idea. You and the dog are vulnerable out there in the open."

"Luna is a K-9 cop and I'm a state trooper. We are both very well trained. I'm sure we'll be fine." The stubborn thrust of her chin was back, and he tried not to show his annoyance.

She and the dog had been shot at. Wasn't that enough of a close call?

"Do you mind giving me a lift back?" Everett didn't wait for permission but headed for the passenger side door. He worked with plenty of female officers and trusted them as much as his male counterparts, but he didn't like the idea of Helena going back to the scene of the shooting, alone.

Even with a K-9 partner. The dog couldn't shoot a gun.

Although he'd sensed the animal would have taken a chunk out of him if Helena hadn't called her off.

Luna jumped into the back of the SUV. Turning in his seat, he was impressed with the heating and cooling system, as well as the cold water dispensing device located in the back, ensuring the animal wouldn't become dehydrated.

Helena shot him a withering look as she slid in behind the wheel. Pulling out of the parking space, she said, "Listen, I know you suspect my sister of being involved in some big crime ring, but I'm telling you that isn't Zoe's style."

"You're saying she hasn't been in trouble before?"

"Oh, she's been in trouble." Helena sighed. "But stupid stuff, like shoplifting, disorderly conduct and underage drinking. Nothing like being a willing participant in organized crime."

"I understand you don't want to think the worst about your twin. But I'm afraid your loyalty is misplaced."

Helena didn't answer, her gaze focused on the road. Tour buses were busy this time of the year. The summer months, July in particular, were the height of tourism for Alaska. People came from all over the lower forty-eight and from other countries to experience the last frontier.

Clueless visitors who weren't smart enough to leave their valuables at home. Was that what had drawn Zoe here? He suspected the answer was a resounding yes.

Her radio crackled again. "Find anything, Will?"

"Only if you count bats and other creatures," her teammate responded dryly. "No sign of—"

"Thanks," she said, quickly cutting him off. "I'm with Everett Brand, one of the local cops from Anchorage, so I'll check in with you later, okay?"

"Sounds good. I have to head back to Anchorage anyway...the colonel called to let me know there's a potential drug bust going down."

Before he'd hung up, Will didn't sound as if he'd noticed that anything was amiss. But Everett knew Helena's team member had been about to mention something significant.

He glanced down at the evidence bag hanging from her waistband, then back at the large Norwegian elkhound in the back of the SUV.

"You're searching for Zoe." He felt like an idiot that he hadn't picked up on the fact sooner.

She ignored his remark. "Do you want me to take you all the way to your cabin?"

What he wanted was to go with her, especially if she was going to continue looking for her twin. He knew K-9s had an amazing ability to track people down by following a scent.

Maybe Helena was right in that the shooter had only intended to scare her away from the area. But something in his gut told him the danger was far from over.

His phone signaled an alarm. He pulled the device out of his pocket and scowled at it. "Yes, please. I need to get back. Something triggered the alarm."

"Probably a wild animal." Helena didn't look concerned.

Normally he'd agree, but most of the wildlife roamed away from the cabin, not usually right up to the front door. He tried focusing on the camera he'd installed but it must have been disconnected as he couldn't see a thing.

Not good.

"Which way?" Helena asked as they approached the sloping hill where she'd been targeted.

"Keep going straight, there's a gravel road off to the right about a mile from here."

She arched a delicate brow. "The dirt road leads to your place?"

"Yes." He stared at his phone again. Was he overreacting? If Helena was out here to find Zoe, he intended to be there, too.

The SUV rocked and rolled up the gravel road to his rental cabin. It was located pretty far off the beaten track. Although there were several people, like the rangers, who knew its location.

"Stay here." Without waiting for Helena to bring the SUV to a complete stop, he pushed open the passenger door and jumped out. Two giant steps forward and he was at the front door of the cabin, glancing around expectantly.

Nothing.

Then he noticed the door was ajar. Pulling his service weapon from the pocket of his cargo shorts, he pushed the door open and listened.

Was that—a *baby* crying?

He shook his head, hoping he wasn't losing his mind. Crossing the threshold, he entered the cabin, stumbling to a halt when he saw the infant carrier sitting on his sofa, a pink bag next to it.

Not his imagination. His heart squeezed painfully in his chest, his thoughts going back to those early days after Colin had been born. The crying infant reminded him of his son.

Who had broken into his cabin to leave a baby behind?

TWO

Helena let Luna out of the back of the SUV and put the K-9 on leash. Everett had rushed inside telling her to stay put, but she thought it would be a better idea to check the perimeter of the cabin, to make sure there was nothing amiss.

Luna eagerly went to work, sniffing and checking things out. When her K-9 alerted near the front door of the cabin, her heart nearly stopped.

That couldn't be right. Zoe couldn't have been here. Had Luna gotten her scents mixed up?

Then she heard it. The sound of a baby crying.

Everett had a baby? No, he wouldn't have left a baby alone in the cabin.

Unless he had a wife, too.

For some reason the thought of Everett having a wife and baby was disappointing. And that was silly, since he'd made it his mission to find and arrest her sister.

Helena forced herself to move forward, stepping up and over the threshold. Everett turned to face her, holding a baby in his arms, his expression an odd mix of horror and amazement.

"I didn't realize you had a baby." It was a stupid statement, but she couldn't seem to think clearly. Blame it on being shot at.

"Not mine, *yours*." Everett shifted the child in his arms, cradling the baby dressed in pink so that she rested against his shoulder, and handed a note to her.

She blinked. Read the note once then yet again, to make sure she wasn't hallucinating.

Officer Brand,
I'm in terrible danger. My baby isn't safe.
Please take her to my sister, Helena, who
is also a cop. Everything you need is in
the pink bag. Tell Christine and Helena
that I'm sorry—and that I love them more
than anything.
Zoe

Luna pressed against her, as if sensing her distress. She glanced at Everett. "Zoe had a baby?"

"She must have." The way he held the baby

bespoke of experience. "From the note, I take it the baby's name is Christine."

"She named the baby after our mother." Helena couldn't believe Zoe'd had a child without telling her. Or their parents, although they'd been living in Arizona for several years and hadn't been back to Alaska recently. Still, a baby was a big deal. "Zoe is in deep trouble, isn't she?"

"Yes." Everett moved forward and began to hand the infant over to her. Christine took exception to the move and began to cry. He quickly reversed his decision, cradling her against his chest again, looking comically bemused. "I need you to take the baby."

"Maybe you and your wife should keep her for a short while." Helena wanted nothing more than to spend time with the niece she hadn't known she'd had, but what would she do with the baby when she was out searching for her sister?

What in the world had Zoe been thinking?

"I don't have a wife." Everett's tone was sharp. "And the note clearly says for you to take the baby."

Yet he was the one holding Christine as if he knew what he was doing.

She rested her hand on Luna's silky head. "Okay, look, can we agree on one thing?"

Everett eyed her warily, swaying slightly from side to side to calm the baby. "Like what?"

She glanced at the note one more time then let out her breath in a silent sigh. "Zoe's in danger. You've already told me that you suspect she's working with a large crime ring."

"Yes, that's my theory," he admitted gruffly.

"Don't you think the best chance of finding Zoe is by working together?"

Everett's gaze dropped to Luna then back up to her. "You were using your K-9 partner to track Zoe."

"Yes. And Luna alerted outside your cabin, indicating my sister was here. Which we know, because she obviously broke in and left Christine behind."

"That's correct, although I have no idea how she found this place," Everett said with a frown.

"Your name is on the rental agreement, I'm sure. And it's likely the locals know that you're here each year," she pointed out.

"It's still well off the beaten path. We need to continue tracking Zoe. I doubt the baby has been here very long." Everett looked at Luna with a new appreciation. "Time is of the essence."

"I agree and am willing to head out to see if Luna can pick up Zoe's scent." She hesitated before adding, "But you'll need to stay here with Christine."

"Me?" A flicker of panic hit his dark eyes, but then he looked again at Luna. Apparently his trust in her K-9's skills outweighed his reluctance to stay behind. "Okay, fine. Go."

A rumble of thunder echoed in the distance. The storm clouds she'd noticed earlier were swirling closer now, likely bringing rain.

Everett was right. Time was running out. Luna could track in the rain, but the threat of lighting was something Helena couldn't ignore.

Helena headed for the door, stopped then turned and crossed to smooth a hand over Christine's caramel-colored hair. She pressed a quick kiss to the baby's scalp before moving away. "Come, Luna."

More thunder rumbled as she and her K-9 stood outside Everett's cabin. With the threat of rain, she grabbed her state trooper hat from the vehicle. Offering the evidence bag containing Zoe's scarf once again, she gave Luna the command.

"Seek. Seek Zoe."

Luna quickly located Zoe's scent at the door to Everett's cabin. Helena guided the dog away and repeated the command.

Luna lifted her nose to the air and moved in a zigzag pattern until she caught the scent. Fat raindrops fell, but Helena ignored them, following Luna as she headed down the gravel drive leading away from the cabin.

Before reaching the road, however, the K-9 turned to the right. Helena noticed the matted grass, as if someone had come through this way recently.

Disregarding the buzz of mosquitos and flies, she followed Luna, hoping and praying that she might find her sister holed up somewhere nearby.

Luna took a winding path then alerted at a fallen tree roughly fifty yards from Everett's cabin.

"Good girl, Luna. Good girl." She gave Luna a quick rub and a treat, imagining Zoe pausing at the fallen tree to rest, maybe tired from lugging the infant carrier. "Seek. Seek Zoe."

Luna leaped up and over the fallen log, leaving Helena to scramble over it in an effort to keep up. The rain was coming down harder now, and she began to shiver.

More thunder rumbled, louder this time. She glanced apprehensively up at the sky. No lightening yet, but for how much longer?

Luna went farther up to the road and alerted again. But then she turned in a circle, whining a little. Helena pushed her damp hair from her face. "What is it, girl? What's wrong?"

Her K-9 partner went back to the spot near the side of the road, where she'd last alerted to Zoe's scent.

Helena rewarded her K-9, even though she was disappointed. Luna had lost the scent. Helena had to believe someone had picked Zoe up, maybe even carried her away from the area.

Lightening shot across the sky. She knew that pushing forward in the middle of a thunderstorm wasn't smart. Reluctantly, she turned and retraced their steps back to Everett's cabin.

Zoe had been so close. How had they missed her?

And where was her twin now?

Everett stared out the window at the rain, trying not to remember how he'd held his son in this very same spot, looking out at a similar storm while his wife slept.

Precious memories that still held the power to slice him like a knife.

Christine had fallen asleep on his shoulder, but when he'd tried to place the baby back in her infant carrier seat, she'd started to cry. Leaving him little choice but to continue holding her while battling the painful memories of the past.

He didn't want to be responsible for a baby. Frankly, he didn't particularly want to work with Helena to find Zoe. But what choice did he have? Zoe was involved in the burglary ring, and Luna could find her.

The baby really put a crimp in his plans.

Yet the sweet scent of baby shampoo made it difficult for him to hang on to his anger. As much as he wanted to be upset with Zoe, he was secretly glad she'd gotten the baby out of harm's way. This innocent little girl shouldn't be anywhere near a group of criminals.

Although he'd rather she had found someone else—*anyone* else—to leave the baby with besides him.

Why had Zoe chosen him? Because she'd seen him here in Denali and assumed that a cop would have connections with the K-9 Unit? Her note indicated she'd known they were both in law enforcement.

Regardless, he knew he couldn't do this. He couldn't handle taking care of a baby. Helena would have to take the baby with her. That was the only solution. She was the baby's aunt, after all, and he was just a cop who intended to arrest Zoe and those she worked for.

The baby wasn't his responsibility.

So why was he standing here, looking out at a rainstorm, holding her?

Another rumble of thunder echoed overhead, causing Christine to startle. Without thinking, he brought his hand up to smooth it over the baby's back.

"Shh, it's okay. You're fine. Go back to sleep."

He didn't like the idea of Helena and Luna being out in the storm. Could a dog track a scent in the rain? He had no idea.

He told himself he only needed Helena to return so she could take the baby and leave, but he also wanted very much to find Zoe.

If Helena's twin was in danger, he couldn't simply turn his back on her. Despite the crimes Zoe had likely committed, she deserved a chance to turn herself in. And if she provided key evidence against the person in charge of the crime ring, then he was fairly certain the district attorney would cut her a deal.

But first they had to find her.

Luna's bark had him turning from the window. He quickly crossed over to the front door and opened it in time to see a very drenched Helena and dog coming toward the cabin.

"Come up with anything?" He held the door open with one hand, so she and Luna could enter.

"We lost her scent about fifty yards from here." Helena stood just inside the doorway, glancing around uncertainly.

"You're soaked. I'll get some towels." Before he could move, Luna shook her body with vigor, spraying him and everything within ten feet with water that had soaked into her fur.

He wiped at his face, wondering how he'd gotten himself into this mess. The baby, the woman, the dog.

It was all too much.

"Sorry about that," Helena said with a grimace.

He sighed. "It's not the dog's fault." Still holding Christine, he moved away to grab towels from the bathroom. When he handed them to Helena, she used one on the dog first, before lifting the other up to dry her hair.

If she treated Christine the same way she'd just treated her K-9 partner, putting the dog's needs before her own, the baby would be just fine.

As if hearing his thoughts, the infant began to cry in earnest. He rocked her back and forth without success.

"Maybe she's hungry?" Helena draped the damp towels over the backs of two chairs and then went over to open the pink bag. She pulled out a can of powdered formula and a bottle. She peered at the label of the formula, reading the instructions.

"Take her." He forced himself to thrust the crying baby into Helena's arms. "I'll make it."

"You seem to know a lot about caring for a baby." Helena paced the length of the cabin, trying to soothe the infant.

He ignored her remark as he filled the bottle with warm water then dissolved the appropriate amount of formula from the can.

"How old do you think she is?"

"Three months, according to the birth certificate I found in the pink bag."

Helena glanced up. "Does the birth certificate list the father's name?"

"Nope." Shaking the bottle vigorously, he returned to where she was standing. "Here, try this."

"Me?" Her voice squeaked a bit.

"Yes. Sit down and hold her in the crook of your arm." His fingers itched to take the baby so he could feed her, but he reminded himself that Christine wasn't his responsibility.

Helena needed to figure out how to take care of her sister's baby, sooner rather than later.

A bolt of lightning zipped across the sky followed by a loud rumble of thunder. The rain picked up, battering the top of his cabin like stones falling from an avalanche.

Peering out the window, he couldn't see the large pine tree he knew was located just a few yards away because of the deluge.

Not good. He glanced back at Helena. She'd

used one of the towels to prevent the baby from resting against her wet clothes and had tossed her trooper hat aside as she fed the infant. The dog, Luna, was curled up at her feet. He grimly realized there was no way in the world they were going anywhere anytime soon.

Rubbing the back of his neck, Everett swallowed a groan.

He didn't want houseguests. He didn't entertain, *ever*. But it didn't matter. He resigned himself to finding Helena some dry clothes and to raid his kitchen to figure out what to make for dinner.

Maybe the storm would blow over soon, enabling them to leave. The good thing about July in Alaska was that the sun stayed out nearly all night.

Except when you couldn't see the sun, like in the middle of a thunderstorm.

Muttering to himself, he went to find sweatpants and a T-shirt for Helena to wear in place of her damp and likely uncomfortable uniform. He set them beside her on the sofa.

"For when you're finished."

"Thanks." Her gaze was focused on Christine. "She's beautiful, isn't she?"

They were both beautiful. His throat closed for a moment, making it impossible to breathe.

"Yeah," he managed to choke out before high-tailing it into the kitchen.

There was ground beef in the fridge and the makings of a salad. Burgers cooked in a fry-pan rather than on the grill would have to do.

He set about preparing the meal, keeping a wary eye on the storm outside. Summer storms tended to blow through quickly, but this seemed to be sticking around longer than he liked.

"Everett? I think she's finished eating."

Drying his hands on a dish towel, he returned to the main living area. "Did you burp her?"

Her eyes widened. "No."

"Put her up against your shoulder and rub her back. Babies think they're full but often there's just a big air bubble in their stomach that needs to be let out."

Helena did as he suggested. "I really think she's full—" She stopped when Christine let out a loud belch. "Well, maybe not."

The corner of his mouth kicked up in a reluctant smile. "Try to give her a little more formula."

"Okay. Hear that, missy? Everett says you need to drink a little more."

The way Helena looked cooing down at the baby was like a sucker punch to the gut. For a brief moment, he saw his wife and their son sitting just like that the last time they were here.

Closing his eyes against the shaft of pain, he turned and stumbled back to the kitchen.

He gripped the edge of the counter with both hands, trying to keep himself centered. His family was gone. Forever.

Helena and Christine weren't his responsibility. They'd return home soon enough.

Leaving him alone. The way he preferred.

He wasn't sure how long he stood there but straightened when he heard Helena address him.

"Everett?"

It took all his willpower to turn to face her and the baby. "What?"

"Will you take her so I can change?"

He found himself walking toward her then abruptly stopping. "Set her in the infant seat, she should be fine."

"Okay." Helena did as he suggested, scooping the clothes from the sofa. "Thanks. I really appreciate this."

He nodded. "I'm making hamburgers and a salad for dinner. If you're hungry."

"I'm famished," she admitted. "Sounds great." Helena hesitated then set the dry clothing down with a rueful glance at herself. "As long as I'm wet, I may as well go outside in the rain to get Luna's dishes and food."

No! He wanted more than anything to shout

at the top of his lungs that he did not want her to make herself at home. But, of course, he didn't say that. Especially since the shooter was still on the loose.

"Would you like me to do that for you?"

"No, my partner is my responsibility."

Her tone was firm, so he nodded. "Okay."

Helena slipped out the door and closed it behind her. Glancing at the baby, he knew he couldn't live with himself if he made another costly mistake. Better that Helena and Christine stay here for a bit longer, than risk them ending up in harm's way.

"Bah-bahbah."

Luna rose and nuzzled the baby as if sensing it was her duty to watch over the child while Helena was outside.

Fine with him. He went into the kitchen to make the salad. When that was finished, he began cooking the burgers.

Luna growled low in her throat, softly at first then progressively louder.

Everett glanced up with a frown, belatedly realizing that Helena hadn't come back inside yet.

A sense of panic hit hard. He removed the frying pan from the stove and quickly went through the living room to where Luna stood growling at the door. He didn't have experience working with K-9s but that didn't stop him from trying.

"Stay, Luna," he said as he opened the door.

The Norwegian elkhound used her muscled bulk to push him out of the way, squeezing through the opening and running outside before he could stop her.

"Luna! Helena? Are you okay?"

No response.

The back of the SUV was open, but he couldn't see Helena anywhere. Had someone grabbed her?

Luna began barking, short staccato barks that portrayed a sense of urgency.

Everett rushed out into the rain, heading for Luna. The animal was standing near the SUV.

As he grew close, he saw Helena's still form on the ground, her skin pale. His heart squeezed tightly. She didn't move, despite the rain pelting her.

"Good girl," he said to Luna as he bent and scooped Helena into his arms. He quickly carried her inside, setting her gently on the sofa.

"Helena? Can you hear me?" He placed his palm against her cheek, willing her to open her eyes.

Luna pressed her nose against Helena's shoulder, as if also encouraging her to wake up.

He quelled a rising panic. He was a cop,

trained to function in an emergency. He needed to get her to a doctor. But where? The park rangers had a first-aid station. Would that be enough?

The nearest full-service hospital was in Anchorage, which was well over four hours away on a good day.

Not in the middle of a thunderstorm.

Helena let out a moan, lifting her hand to her head. "What happened?"

The tightness in his chest eased a bit when she spoke. "I was hoping you could tell me."

Her brow furrowed and she moved her hand to the back of her head. "Someone came up behind me…and hit me hard. That's all I can remember—"

Because she'd been knocked unconscious.

Everett gently palpated the back of her head, feeling a lump the size of a robin's egg beginning to form. No blood, thankfully, which meant she had a hard head.

He battled a wave of anger. First the shooting on the hill and now this.

What was going on here?

Zoe being in trouble was one thing, but these attacks on Helena seemed…*personal.*

He didn't like this turn of events one bit. And silently vowed to protect Helena and Christine.

No matter the cost to him emotionally.

THREE

Her head throbbed from where she'd been struck from behind, but she was more upset about allowing someone to sneak up on her in the first place, catching her off guard.

She was a cop and had made a naïve mistake in thinking they were safe here at the cabin while in the middle of a thunderstorm. Even though she'd suspected someone had picked up Zoe from the area less than an hour ago.

Stupid, Helena mentally berated herself. She should have known better.

"Are you sure you're okay?" Everett's dark eyes clung to hers. "I still think we should go to the nearest health clinic."

Everett's concern only made her more upset at herself. Would he be this attentive if she were a male counterpart? Would he have carried a man inside?

Ha! Not likely.

"No need, I'm fine." She forced the words

through gritted teeth. "I'd like to change into dry clothes now, if you don't mind."

"Sure." He looked uncertain for a moment. "I'll get Luna's dishes. What do they look like?"

"No, let me get them." It was important for her to provide for her K-9 partner, but the pain was bad enough that she would have preferred staying right where she was.

"But—"

"Don't worry, I'll take Luna with me." The way she should have in the first place. If she'd had Luna at her side, her partner would have alerted her to an impending attack. "Luna will only take food and water from me, not a stranger."

He looked surprised "Good to know. Oh, the burgers are done."

She drew a deep breath and forced herself to sit upright. The room spun crazily before righting itself. "I'll be ready in fifteen minutes."

"Okay." Everett moved back into the kitchen.

She stood, resting her hand lightly on Luna's head for support, and warmth flowed through her as Christine made more gurgling noises. The baby was happy, and she found herself amazed that Zoe had actually gotten pregnant and given birth without calling her.

Difficult to wrap her head around the fact that her twin was a mother.

"Come, Luna." Moving gingerly, she made her way outside. Standing beneath the over-hang, she swept her gaze over the area, search-ing for any sign of someone lurking nearby, before once again approaching the SUV.

"Guard." The dog lifted her nose and moved closer to Helena's side.

Reaching into the back hatch, she quickly grabbed the stainless-steel dog dishes and bucket of kibble. Securing both, she shut the SUV and returned to the cabin, unable to resist a furtive glance over her shoulder. Although it was useless. Seeing anything through the del-uge was nearly impossible.

Inside, Helena used the same towel she had earlier to dry off, grimacing as Luna once again shook herself, spraying water everywhere. Then she took the food and water dishes into the kitchen and set them in the corner of the room. After filling Luna's water dish, Helena led the K-9 over. The animal hesitated for only a moment before lapping at the water and then moving over to eat her food.

"Good girl," she said in a low voice. Wincing as each step made her head hurt, she carefully made her way into the living room. Scooping the dry clothing off the sofa, she found the bath-room and changed out of her soggy uniform.

Wearing dry things was wonderful, although

it wasn't easy to ignore the hint of Everett's pine-scented aftershave lingering in the fabric. She was more aware of him than she should be.

"Dinner's ready," he said when she emerged a few minutes later.

Helena wanted nothing more than to close her eyes and rest, but showing weakness wasn't an option. She was a cop and needed to be strong.

Her former fiancé, Kade, hadn't liked that she was a state trooper and therefore often in danger. He had begged her to find a different line of work, anything that wouldn't cause her to be placed in harm's way. At first she'd thought his concern was sweet, but eventually realized that her ex wasn't being protective as much as he simply didn't trust her.

He hadn't appreciated her skill and training, or her ability to take care of herself. And he hadn't trusted that God was watching over her.

And maybe her being in law enforcement and able to take down men twice her size had threatened his masculinity in some weird way. When he'd given her a choice between him and her career, she hadn't thought twice. She'd chosen her career.

It was never easy being a woman in a man's world. She'd worked hard for this position in the K-9 team, and she wasn't going to give that up for anyone.

The State Trooper K-9 Unit had become her family. They helped solve crimes across the large state of Alaska, working with local and federal law enforcement agencies. There were several members of the team, each of them paired with K-9's with different areas of expertise. Hunter McCord and his Siberian Husky, Juneau, specialized in search and rescue. Poppy Walsh and her Irish wolfhound partner Stormy ran down poachers. Maya Rodriguez and her Malinois, Sarge, screened for weapons and explosives. Sean West and his Akita, Grace, searched for cadavers—one of the hardest roles in Helena's opinion. Braydon Ford and his Newfoundland, Ella, could do underwater search and rescue, and Gabriel Runyon and his Saint Bernard, Bear, rounded out the team with in-snow detection.

They each had earned their place on the team, and she enjoyed being part of the K-9 family. Reminding herself she was a cop and could handle a small knock on the head, she crossed the room to sit at the table. Luna came over and nudged her hand, begging for attention rather than food. She ruffled the dog's still damp fur, then told her to lie down. The K-9 obediently stretched out on the floor at her feet.

"That dog is extremely well behaved," Everett said, handing her a plate.

"Extremely well *trained*," she corrected.

"How long have you worked with Luna?" He set a plate of burgers on the table, along with condiments and a large salad.

"Just over four years."

He nodded and took the seat across from her. She took a moment to bow her head, silently thanking God for keeping them all safe, for guiding Zoe to leave Christine with them, and for the food Everett had cooked for her. When she opened her eyes and lifted her head, she noticed he was sitting very still, waiting for her to finish.

"Looks delicious, thank you." Her stomach churned a bit with nausea, but she ignored it.

"You're welcome." An awkward silence fell between them and she wondered where he'd learned to care for a baby and why he didn't have a family.

The way he'd told her he wasn't married had seemed…well, blunt—almost bordering on rude. As if she'd poked at a sore tooth.

Not her problem. The only reason she and Everett were working together was to find Zoe and because of the baby.

As if on cue, Christine began to fuss. Before she could move, Everett was up and heading into the other room. When he returned, he had Christine tucked against him, so that the baby was facing outward, gazing around with frank interest.

"She seems fine now." Helena eyed her niece thoughtfully.

"Likes having people around, that's all." He ate one-handed, the other holding the baby.

The burly man and cute baby were adorable together.

By the time they'd finished eating, Helena's head was pounding so hard she could barely see straight. Everett must have noticed because he gestured toward the living room.

"Lie down on the sofa for a while. I have over the counter pain meds if you'd like them. You're in no shape to search for Zoe."

"I'm fine," she said, even though she really wasn't. "Although the pain meds would be great."

"I'll get them for you. Rest while I clean up."

A short nap sounded wonderful, so she did as he suggested, moving her trooper hat so she could stretch out on the couch. He gave her the meds, which she downed with water. Luna padded over to her hand, which made her smile.

Her eyes drifted closed and her last conscious thought was that it had been a long time since anyone had taken care of her without judging her career choices or blaming her for being in the situation in the first place.

And it felt nice.

Everett jiggled Christine on his knee as he finished his salad.

Helena's green eyes had been shadowed with pain and she'd only eaten half her burger. That was better than nothing, but it worried him that her concussion might be far worse than he'd originally believed. He should drive Helena to the hospital, where they would likely do a CT scan of her head and keep her overnight for observation.

He glanced down at the baby sitting on his lap. Christine was a happy kid, patting the table with her hands and babbling nonsensically.

Despite his best effort to convince himself otherwise, the baby was clearly his responsibility.

At least, for now. Helena needed to rest and recuperate.

Shifting the baby up and into the crook of his arm, he began cleaning off the table one-handed. After a few minutes, he went to retrieve the infant carrier seat and brought it into the kitchen so he could put Christine down in a position where she could sit and watch him.

Luna had stretched out on the floor in front

of the sofa, as if to guard Helena. Once again, he was impressed with how well the K-9 behaved. Or had been *trained*, as Helena had pointed out. He'd never really realized how much of a true partnership a K-9 had with its handler.

For a brief instant, the idea of getting a dog crossed his mind, but he ruthlessly shoved it away. As a cop, he worked long hours, he wasn't home enough to take care of a dog.

Besides, he couldn't handle being responsible for another living creature.

Present baby, injured trooper and K-9 aside.

He blew out a breath. When Helena had prayed before their meal, he'd been taken back to those early days of his marriage. He and Sheila had attended church regularly, believing God was watching over them.

But when he'd lost his family, he'd lost his faith. Oh, he still believed in God, but Everett didn't think that He cared about him or his family.

God certainly hadn't protected Sheila and Colin from the drug addict who'd shot them.

Frankly, Everett had been unable to tolerate attending church after their funerals. The memory was too fresh and raw.

Even now, just the idea of being inside a church made him break out in a cold sweat.

Enough. No reason to rehash the past. He needed to focus on the next steps of the investigation.

By the time he'd finished cleaning up the kitchen and washing the dishes, the rain was beginning to let up. Instead of coming down in droves it was now a light, soothing sprinkle. Dark clouds still hovered overhead, even though the sun wouldn't set for hours yet.

Christine began to fuss again, so he picked her up and walked in circles, the way he used to with Colin. As he soothed the baby, he wondered about the attack on Helena on the heels of her and Luna's attempt to track Zoe.

He paused to stare out the window. Was someone still hanging around out there somewhere? And if so, why? What good would it do to take Helena out of the investigation when he was still actively working the case?

Was that why Zoe had left Christine here? As a way to distract him? No, she had to know that if anything happened to him or to Helena, this little girl would end up a ward of the state.

A grim thought.

He'd suspected that maybe one of the hotels at the base of Denali might be Zoe's next target. But which one? And which event? There were many things going on in the height of the tourist season.

And how did these attacks on Helena fit in? Considering she'd been wearing her uniform both times, the attacker couldn't have mistaken Helena for Zoe.

Christine had fallen asleep in his arms. Her sweet face was so innocent, he couldn't help but smile at how she looked resting against him.

His heart squeezed painfully as he relived the loss of his family. He'd had all of this once.

And had lost it in a heartbeat.

He gently set Christine back in her carrier. Glancing at Helena, who was also sleeping, he decided a walk would do him good.

Not just to put some distance between himself and this pseudo family he'd been saddled with. Checking the perimeter was important; maybe he'd find some clues as to who had attacked Helena.

It made sense that the shooter and the attacker was the same perp.

Spurred with a renewed sense of purpose, he fastened his shoulder holster then pulled on his rain slicker. He also grabbed a flashlight, because the storm clouds made it difficult to see in some areas.

Luna lifted her head, gazing at him with curious, dark eyes.

"Stay," he whispered. "Guard," he added, unsure if that was even a command the animal understood.

Luna continued watching him as he quietly left the cabin. For some reason, he felt guilty tiptoeing away, which was ridiculous. If Christine began to cry, Helena would hear her and so would Luna. They would be fine.

No reason to hover over them while they slept.

Outside, the rain had cleansed the air, leaving a fresh scent behind. Even with the dark clouds swirling in the sky, the areas of the mountain that he could see were stunning.

This was the part of being in Alaska that he loved.

He inspected the ground around the back of Helena's K-9 SUV. There were a lot of footprints in the muddied ground, but nothing distinctive, from what he could see.

Everett widened his search area, trying to figure out if there was a distinct path the attacker had taken.

The rain slowed even further until it became a fine mist. As he was about to turn back to the cabin, he noticed a thread hanging from a thorny bush.

Crouching, he played his flashlight over the thread. Could this have been here for days, or even a week? Doubtful. He pulled a baggie out of the pocket of his rain slicker and put the thread inside, even though he knew it might not be significant.

Another few feet away, he found a footprint and a cigarette butt. The butt could have DNA evidence or a fingerprint, so he placed that carefully in another evidence bag. The toe of the print was pointing in the general direction of the front door of the cabin.

The tread looked to be that of a hiking shoe. Using his own foot as an estimate, he decided the owner was a man wearing a size twelve shoe.

Could be a woman, he supposed, but not likely. Zoe was small, like Helena. They believed three men were orchestrating the thefts around Anchorage, along with Zoe, who allegedly was in a relationship with one of the guys involved. Unfortunately, Everett didn't know who.

Had the crime ring moved to Denali? They'd already hit two weddings, an anniversary party and a retirement party.

They preferred cash—didn't everyone? But would also take jewelry or any other small, easy-to-carry valuables. And the last heist after the anniversary party had included a large diamond ring and several gold chains left on the dresser in a guest room, accessed by one of the maid's master keys. He suspected Zoe had presented herself as the maid.

None of the goods had showed up at any local pawn shops. At least, not yet.

Galvanized by finding clues, he continued searching, taking the route he now believed the assailant had used to approach the cabin.

When he realized he'd been gone the better part of an hour, Everett turned and headed back to the cabin. He took his time, keeping a keen eye out for additional clues. Finding another hiking shoe print, he took a moment to photograph that one, too, making a note in his phone about roughly where it was located.

Rocking back on his heels, he realized this was a footprint headed away from the cabin. The perp hadn't used the same route back and forth.

Interesting. Did this mean the guy was familiar with the area?

As he came around a large bush, he caught a glimpse of something blue moving up ahead. His pulse skyrocketed. Someone was heading to the cabin!

He drew his weapon and broke into a run. Growing closer, he could see a man creeping up to the back of his place, toward one of the windows there. He was still far away, but that didn't keep Everett from shouting, "Stop! Police!"

The perp swung around and in a heartbeat several things registered at once. The guy wasn't in uniform but wore a frayed denim jacket and blue jeans. And he was armed. The gun swung toward Everett. He threw himself sideways, hit the ground and rolled as the gunshot echoed around him.

Everett kept his head down, bracing himself for more gunfire. Hearing nothing, he gingerly lifted up onto his elbows, his weapon ready.

The guy was gone.

No! He couldn't let him get away. Everett lurched to his feet and ran for the cabin, raking his gaze over the area.

There was no sign of him.

He continued in the direction he felt certain the perp had gone. But after fifteen minutes of seeing nothing, he stopped.

Better to go back to the cabin, make sure Helena and the baby were okay.

Dejected, he headed back. He'd just lost the best lead they'd had to find Zoe.

FOUR

Helena had woken to the sound of Luna's growling and gunfire. After instinctively tucking Christine's infant carrier behind the sofa and commanding Luna to guard her, she'd tried to figure out what was going on.

There had been no sign of Everett and she was deeply concerned that he might be lying injured somewhere in the woods. But she didn't dare leave Christine alone, or take the baby along, into possible danger, to search for him.

Should she send Luna? It was an option, but one she didn't relish. Yet, what else could she do? Sitting here and waiting, basically doing nothing, was making her antsy. She paced from window to window, peering out while hoping and praying Everett was alive and unharmed.

Then she saw him, jogging toward the cabin. Heaving a sigh of relief, she went to open the door.

"What happened?" She raked him with a keen gaze. No injuries, from what she could see.

"I lost him." Disgust tinged his tone.

"Who?"

He shook his head. "I was searching the area around the cabin for clues and caught a glimpse of a man wearing a blue denim jacket. He was lurking behind the cabin, trying to peer into the window."

Helena's pulse jumped. "Did you recognize him?"

"No." Everett blew out a breath. "I told him to stop and identified myself as a cop, but he turned, shot at me, then took off running. I gave chase but lost him."

Helena rubbed her temple, doing her best to ignore the lingering pain in her head. "I wish I had been there to send Luna after him. She'd have brought him down in a heartbeat."

Hearing her name, the dog came out from behind the sofa. Realizing Christine was still back there, Helena crossed over to lift the carrier. The sofa hadn't offered much protection, but it was all she'd had. Luna nudged her, wagging her bushy tail.

"Okay, so now what?" Helena tried to concentrate on the case. "Why would some guy be lurking outside the cabin?"

"Maybe he was looking for Zoe?"

She considered Everett's theory. "Meaning she escaped from the crime ring and they want her back? It would explain why she dropped Christine off here. Easier to go on the run without lugging a baby around."

"True," Everett agreed. "I found several other clues, as well."

When he explained what he'd found, Helena couldn't help being impressed with Everett's tracking abilities. "The prints from the hiking boot were at the back of the cabin, despite the way I tracked Zoe in the front of the cabin, heading to the road."

"Yeah." Everett looked thoughtful. "The guy in the denim jacket could very well have been searching for Zoe."

"Maybe. Or he's the same one who fired at me earlier, when I was on the hill. And was also responsible for hitting me over the head and knocking me out." Helena was having trouble putting all the puzzle pieces together. "The more I think about it, I'm the likely target in all this."

"But why?" Everett frowned. "It doesn't make any sense to go after you. And the guy who tried to shoot you earlier used a rifle—I recognized the sound. The perp at the window used a handgun. And if they wanted you dead, why simply club you in the head and leave you in the rain? Why not shoot you and be done with it?"

"Crooks often have more than one weapon, and maybe they don't want me dead. Maybe they're coming after me because they think I know where Zoe is." Helena rubbed her temple again. "Regardless of who might be the target, we can't stay here."

He exhaled roughly. "You're right. The guy in the blue shirt or any of his cohorts in crime could come back any time."

"I'd like to stay in Denali, but it's the height of the tourist season. Do you think we'll be able to find another rental?"

"Doubtful." Everett shrugged. "We can ask the park rangers to see if they have any leverage to get us one. I need to drop this evidence off to them, anyway."

"Let me call my boss. She has the most leverage of anyone I know." Helena put a call in to the colonel, surprised when Lorenza herself answered in a crisp voice. "Gallo."

"Colonel? It's Helena. I need a favor." In her experience, it was always best to get to the point.

"You've found your sister?" Lorenza asked.

"Not yet." She glanced at Christine. "But Everett Brand, a cop with the Anchorage Police Department, and I are working together to find her. Zoe left her baby in our care, so we know she's here in Denali, in the same general area Eli picked up her last cell transmission."

"Wow. A baby?" Her boss's tone rose incredulously.

"Not only that," Helena went on, "but someone took a shot at me, then attacked and knocked me unconscious, and most recently fired a gun at Officer Brand. We're in a rental cabin but need another place to stay as soon as possible. Any chance you can hook us up with something nearby?"

"Are you sure you're okay?" Trust the colonel to focus in on a possible injury to one of her team members. The Alaska K-9 Unit didn't just work together, they were family.

"I have a headache, but am otherwise fine, thanks. And so is Officer Brand." Helena glanced at Everett, who'd picked up Christine as she'd begun to fuss. The way he comforted the baby, made her heart turn to mush. "Any place in the general area of Denali should work."

"Okay, give me a minute."

She could hear the muffled sounds of a keyboard as Lorenza searched.

"Helena? There's a vacation rental that you can use under the name of Myles Campton. It's vacant for the week. Is that enough time?"

"Yes, that's great. Thanks." She was grateful for her boss's extensive connections. One of the benefits of working law enforcement for so many years.

"I'll send you the address and the location to find the key," Lorenza continued. "And I'm sending Will back to act as an escort. He ended up sheltering in one of the small towns along the way when the storm hit."

"Sounds good. I wouldn't mind extra help, considering we have a baby to look after."

"Okay, stay put while I send him your location. And let me know if you need additional backup. You know any of the team members will be happy to assist."

"I know, but they're also working other cases, not to mention searching for Violet James, our missing bride," Helena pointed out. The bride had been missing since April and still hadn't been found, despite the team's efforts in searching for her. "We'll be okay."

"If you need anything else, I'm just a phone call away."

"Thanks again." Helena disconnected, smiling as she noticed how Everett was swaying from side to side to soothe Christine. "We have a new place to stay, and one of my team members, Will Stryker, will be here to protect us. Let's pack up so we're ready to go when he arrives."

"Sounds good," Everett agreed.

Thankfully, the baby's stuff was easily packed in the pink diaper bag Zoe had left with them. Helena kept her weapon in one hand with Luna at her side, as she carried the bag and the dog's food and dishes outside to her SUV.

The area around the cabin appeared deserted, but she wasn't taking any chances. Luna didn't growl, adding reassurance they were alone. She returned to the cabin to find Everett packing food in several large canvas bags. "This will just go bad if we leave it behind."

She nodded. "Agree. Oh, and I need my uniform, too."

"Here, take the food, and I'll pack a duffel of clothing for us to wear."

As Helena took the food out to the SUV, she heard the sound of a car engine. She tensed then relaxed when she saw the K-9 SUV.

"Hear you've had more trouble," Will said by way of greeting.

"A little." She smiled at Will's border collie, Scout. "Glad you're able to provide an extra layer of security for us."

"Not a problem." Will's expression turned grave. "I heard about Zoe's baby. Are you doing okay?"

Helena forced a smile. "How can I be upset about a baby? Christine is adorable." Her smile faded. "We need to find Zoe."

"And arrest her," he added dryly.

She bristled. "It's innocent until proven guilty, Stryker. Not the other way around. Your unwillingness to remember that is going to get you into trouble one day."

He shrugged. "Okay, okay."

Helena knew Will had trust issues, but before she could say anything more, Everett joined them.

"I'm ready." Everett was carrying Christine's infant carrier with one hand and a duffel bag slung over his shoulder.

"Okay, then let's go." Helena turned to her colleague. "Follow us?"

"Absolutely."

Helena watched, impressed by the way Everett easily buckled Christine and her infant carrier into the back passenger seat. When he climbed in beside her, she pulled up the information Lorenza had sent to her phone and plugged it into the vehicle's GPS.

The cabin was located on the other side of Denali, but no closer to the hotels, which might have been helpful.

Leaving the last place she knew that Zoe had been wasn't easy. Was her sister somewhere safe?

Or still in the crosshairs of danger?

Please, God, keep Zoe safe in Your caring hands.

* * *

Everett glanced at Helena, curious about her conversation with her boss. "You mentioned that missing bride case." Everett had taken a detour to drop off the evidence at the park ranger station but was now only fifteen minutes from the cabin. "Is that investigation still going on?" Being a cop in Anchorage, he knew about the murder of a local tour guide, hired to take a bridal party out in the wilderness. The bride, Violet James, had gone missing and her groom-to-be, Lance Wells, and his best man, Jared Dennis, were suspected of killing the tour guide and pushing the maid of honor over a cliff. Thankfully, Ariel Potter had survived. The K-9 Unit had been called in to work the case as the crimes had taken place outside local jurisdictions. The bride was from a wealthy family, and Everett had intended to be at the wedding, in case it was a target for the criminal ring.

"Yes, unfortunately. But I'm confident we'll find her. Some of my team members are working very hard, as we believe she's in danger, too."

After seeing the K-9 team in action, he believed her. For the first time, he appreciated how much freedom Helena and her unit had, with their ability to work cases all across the state.

"Christine seems content," Helena said, glancing at the rearview mirror.

"Babies love car rides." The words popped out of his mouth before he could stop them.

"You know an awful lot about babies," she remarked.

A lump rose to his throat. For years, he'd kept his personal life, and his personal loss, private. But for some reason, he was tempted to tell Helena what had happened three years ago.

How he'd lost his wife and young son in the blink of an eye.

Then the moment was gone.

"Isn't that Arch, the park ranger?" Helena asked as they passed a ranger SUV headed in the opposite direction. "They're going to call us when they finish testing the cigarette butt for fingerprints and DNA as soon as possible, right? It would be nice to get a hit through CODIS."

Aware she was referring to the FBI's Combined DNA Index System, he nodded. "They are." Lost in the painful memories of the past, he'd missed seeing the park ranger's vehicle.

He needed to stay focused.

"Tell me why you're so convinced Zoe is guilty of working for the organized crime ring."

Everett glanced at her. "I received a tip from my informant."

"Tip about what?" Helena demanded. "And why is this informant of yours so credible?"

"I know informants can't always be trusted, but this particular guy is a petty criminal I picked up over a week ago. He claims to have seen Zoe handing off a large diamond ring and gold jewelry to a man wearing a baseball cap low over his face. And the reason we believed him was that a diamond ring and gold jewelry were stolen during an anniversary party. We didn't broadcast the information about exactly what was taken, so how else would this guy have known if he hadn't seen the hand-off for himself?"

"He could have heard about it from someone else, but I guess that would still implicate Zoe." She hesitated then asked, "What's the name of the informant?"

He hesitated, as this was information he wouldn't normally share. But she was his partner in this and he needed her to find Zoe. "Norbert Monroe." He watched her expression carefully. "Do you know him?"

"No." Helena looked disappointed. "I wish I did. And you're sure he didn't recognize the guy with the baseball cap?"

"I tried to get a name, without success." He

shrugged. "Was Norbert lying? Maybe. But my gut says no. I think Norbert's the kind of guy who would give the name up if he had it. He's always looking for extra cash."

"Diamond ring and gold jewelry," Helena murmured. He could tell the information bothered her.

"We'll find her," he reassured her.

She nodded but didn't say anything else until they arrived at the new cabin.

"The key should be tucked beneath a loose board," Helena said, gazing at the side of the cabin with a frown.

"Stay here, I'll find it." He pulled his weapon and slid out of the passenger seat. With a quick glance at Christine, who was looking around curiously, he walked quickly up to the front door.

He glanced over his shoulder when Will Stryker's SUV pulled up behind Helena's. Then he turned back toward the cabin and found a spot near the front porch light where the board was raised. Sure enough, the key was tucked underneath. After unlocking the door, he went inside to check the place out.

It was similar to the cabin he'd rented, maybe a little more rustic, but it would work fine for what they needed.

Everett went back outside to find Helena

trying to remove Christine's car seat from the back. He went over to help. "I'll get this, you take care of Luna."

"Thanks." Helena released the rear hatch and the K-9 jumped out, eagerly heading over to meet up with Scout. Luna was much larger, but Scout was scrappy enough to hold his own as they played.

Will offered his assistance in hauling their things inside. It didn't take long to put the food away and have everything else placed neatly in the two bedrooms located off the living room. Helena noticed Everett had forgotten her state trooper hat, but decided there would be time to get it later.

Once the danger was over.

"I think you're set," Will said.

"Thanks for your help." Helena smiled. "I guess it was a good thing you ended up staying nearby to ride out the storm."

"Yes, thanks," Everett added. "It's always good to have backup." A simple thing he hadn't done three years ago.

And had the emotional scars to prove it.

"No problem." Will glanced at Helena. "You need me to stick around awhile?"

"It's getting late," Helena said. "Might be better for you to get some rest and head out in the morning."

"Not like it's dark out," Will countered, gesturing to the brightness through the windows. "Sun doesn't set until midnight these days."

"I know, makes it hard to keep track of the time." Everett glanced at the kitchen. "If you're hungry, we can pull out some snacks."

"Nah, I'm fine. Helena, maybe we should scout the area with our K-9s."

"Not a bad idea." She glanced at Everett. "Will you watch Christine for a while?"

"Sure." It wasn't as if he had a choice. As much as he wanted to assist in checking their surroundings, he couldn't deny the added value of having a K-9 along to perform the task.

Will and Helena left, leaving him alone with the baby. When Christine began to fuss, he realized she was hungry again and thought maybe she'd fall sleep for the rest of the night if he fed her now.

He prepared the bottle then began to feed the baby, thinking of all the times he'd missed feeding his own son. Not that he hadn't tried to do his share, but he'd been working a lot of hours back then, which had left most of the work to Sheila.

It wouldn't be easy working the case while caring for a baby. He thought about handing Christine over to the department of health and human services, but everything inside him recoiled at the idea.

If by some remote possibility Zoe was an innocent pawn in this, she shouldn't be punished for leaving her baby someplace safe. And once Christine was in the system, it would be difficult to get her out.

They'd just have to find a way to make it work.

Helena and Will returned by the time he'd finished feeding and changing Christine. A cell phone dinged with an incoming message, and each instinctively reached for their respective phones. Will frowned. "This is a text from Sean West," he said slowly.

"What happened?" Helena asked.

Will's expression turned serious. "We have a break in the missing bride case. Sean says they received a tip about Lance Wells and his best man, Jared Dennis, being spotted in downtown Anchorage."

Everett's interest peaked. That was his jurisdiction.

"Were they captured?" Helena's expression radiated hope.

"No, and it sounds like they are both to be considered armed and dangerous." Will hesitated then put the phone away. "Scout and I need to head back to assist in tracking them down."

Everett didn't like the idea of these guys being armed and dangerous in his city. "Good idea."

Helena nodded. "Absolutely, Will. We're safe here."

"Thanks. Come, Scout." Will called the dog away from Luna.

"Let me know how it goes," she added.

Will nodded and raised a hand as he left the cabin.

Everett found himself slightly envious about the camaraderie Helena had with the members of the Alaska K-9 Unit. Or maybe he'd just been knocked off balance at how Helena and Will had looked so chummy as they'd worked together.

Jealous? *No way.*

He wasn't interested in falling in love or in having a family of his own again.

Not now, not ever.

FIVE

Sending Will and Scout back to Anchorage to help locate Lance and Jared was the right thing to do. And, truthfully, Helena felt safe in their new cabin, especially with Luna on guard. No one outside the K-9 team members knew their location, which would give them time to come up with another plan to track Zoe.

But spending so much time with Everett and Christine was messing with her head. Obviously, he had experience caring for babies. He knew far more about them than she did. But each time she'd asked about it, he hadn't responded.

Despite her innate curiosity, it was none of her business. Everett Brand was one puzzle she'd have to ignore.

"What do you think?" Everett said, breaking into her thoughts. "Did Lance Wells only propose to Violet because of her father's money?"

She nodded slowly. "That's my belief, yes.

Who has the most to lose in all of this? Lance does. Plus, I interviewed her best friend and bridesmaid, Ariel. She insists Lance and Jared are lying." She hesitated before adding, "I'm not sure if you're aware of the fact that Violet wrote a note proclaiming her innocence." She met his dark brown gaze. "Based on Ariel's testimony and the note, I believe Violet is a victim in this. There's no reason for her to murder anyone."

"I hadn't heard about the letter, but I have to agree with you." He eyed her thoughtfully. "How's your head?"

She shrugged, downplaying the injury. Luna came over to sit at her side. "Not bad."

"I can tell you have a headache, Helena," he said softly. "Get some sleep. I have no idea if Christine will sleep through the night or wake up for a feeding, but I can take care of her if she does."

She glanced at the sleeping baby. "It's okay for her to stay in the carrier?"

"Sure, she's not old enough to roll over yet."

There it was again, the calm voice of experience. He'd refused to answer her twice now, but she felt the need to ask one more time.

"I know it's none of my business, Everett, but I can tell you've taken care of a child in the past." She smiled gently and stroked Luna's soft fur. "If you don't want to talk about it, that's fine. But I'm here if you want to."

He didn't answer for so long, she figured she'd just go into the bedroom to get some rest. As she rose, he said, "I lost my wife and infant son three years ago."

He had? Her knees went weak and she sank back onto the sofa. "Oh, Everett. I'm so sorry for your loss."

"That's what everyone says." He looked past her, his gaze focusing on something far in the distance. "But no one really understands. Losing them was the most awful thing I've lived through. There are no words to describe it."

Her heart squeezed in her chest. She couldn't imagine losing her spouse and infant son. Just thinking of something bad happening to Christine was enough for her to break into a cold sweat. "I agree there are no words. No offer of condolence that will make a difference. I'm sorry you had to live through that terrible tragedy."

"A tragedy? Their deaths were my fault." The words were spoken in a low, harsh tone. "I made a rookie mistake that will haunt me for the rest of my life."

She wanted to ask more, but sensed he was hanging on by a thread. "I don't believe that."

His dark gaze was tortured. "It's true."

Helena held her breath, waiting—*hoping*—he'd explain. She knew she could likely search the internet to learn what had happened, but she didn't want to do that.

"A drug addict broke into the house." The words were halting, as if his voice was rusty. "I tried to talk to him, to get him to surrender his weapon. He was so young, barely old enough to drive."

She had a bad feeling she knew where this was going. "But he didn't give up his weapon."

"No. I should have called for backup right away—that was my second big mistake. As I was talking to him, Sheila came into the room holding Colin. I tried to wave them back, but Sheila must not have noticed. Unfortunately, her presence startled the kid and he fired several shots before I could return fire." He lifted his tortured gaze to hers. "The kid survived, but my wife and son, didn't."

His story was worse than she'd imagined, and she couldn't help wondering if being forced to return fire on the young man had only added to the trauma of losing his family. "It's terrible, Everett, but I don't think trying to talk a kid down is a mistake. And it doesn't sound as if backup would have gotten there in time, either."

"Then why is he alive when my family isn't?" Everett's voice held a note of bitterness.

"Why would God do that, huh? Take a beautiful woman and an infant boy's life and spare that of a drug addict?"

"I know it's not easy to understand God's will," she acknowledged. "It's not up to us to question Him."

"Yeah, well, I don't believe God was watching over us that night. Or any night." He stood. "I need to get some sleep."

Everett disappeared into one of the bedrooms where he'd left his duffel bag.

Helena sat in silence, looking out at the eerily bright sky as she considered his words.

The story of how he'd lost his wife and son was troubling enough. But hearing his view on God and faith was nearly as disheartening.

And she completely understood where he was coming from. Suffering a dual loss like that was heartbreaking. There was no logic in the world to explain the series of events.

But she didn't understand why Everett blamed himself. Given the same set of circumstances, she'd have done the same thing.

Any good cop would try to talk a sixteen-year-old kid into giving up his weapon. It wasn't always easy to understand God's plan. To understand why Everett had lost his family while the young man had survived.

Helena did know, that hearing about Everett's

loss made it impossible to keep her distance from him. He was still the cop who wanted to arrest her sister, but he was also so much more.

He was sweet and protective. Gentle yet strong. For some reason, she felt a strange kinship with him.

Everett Brand might try to arrest her twin, but she also knew with a deep sense of certainty that he'd do anything possible to keep Zoe and her baby safe from harm.

She stood, bent to press a soft kiss on the top of Christine's head and then took Luna outside one last time before heading into her own room.

Exhausted, with a nagging headache, Helena had thought she'd fall asleep instantly. But her deep concern over Everett's pain and lack of faith nagged at her. It wasn't until darkness finally cloaked the sky that she was able to sleep.

Everett heard Christine making soft blathering sounds and skyrocketed out of bed to get her a bottle before the cuteness turned into full-blown wailing.

The sky was bright when he stumbled into the kitchen. Not that a light sky meant anything, sunrise at this time of the year was as early as four o'clock in the morning.

After making the bottle, he went over to pick the

baby up from her carrier. She squirmed and failed her fists, rapping him gently against the chin.

"You're going to need a better fist than that once the boys come calling," he whispered. He finished changing her and gave her a bottle. With one hand, he checked his phone for messages. Nothing from the rangers on the fingerprint or DNA testing.

Helena was still sleeping, which was likely the best thing for her head injury. Gazing down into Christine's wide green eyes, mirror images of Helena's, he couldn't believe he'd spilled his guts about losing his wife and son.

What on earth had he been thinking?

He should have known, especially when Helena had prayed before eating, that she'd talk about God's plan. It was something Sheila would have said, as well.

But he knew differently. There was no such thing as God's plan. Bad stuff happened. People suffered.

End of story.

A strange sound from somewhere outside the cabin caught his attention. He set the baby in her infant seat and grabbed his weapon. Easing outside, he swept a gaze over the area.

He didn't see anyone and walked the perimeter of the cabin just in case. He relaxed when his search came up empty. Probably, just an animal. When he went back inside, he found Helena standing there with Luna.

"I heard you leave. Is something wrong?" She asked with a frown.

"False alarm."

"Luna will let us know for sure." Helena quickly put the dog on a leash and headed outside.

While waiting for her to return, Everett made eggs and toast, hoping Helena liked them scrambled.

"Everything is clear," Helena said as she entered the kitchen and unhooked Luna's leash. "Something smells great. Is there anything I can do?"

"You can make coffee, if you don't mind?" He wondered if she felt awkward around him now that she knew how badly he'd failed his family.

"Coffee is definitely a priority." Helena joined him in the kitchen. "I never heard Christine. Sorry if she woke you."

"I didn't give her time to work into a full-blown crying jag." He continued making the eggs and toast. "She's all fed and changed."

"Thanks for doing that." Helena rested against the counter as the coffee began to brew. "We should probably talk about what our next steps should be in our efforts to locate Zoe."

"Yeah." He was grateful to have the conversation turned toward work. All this domestication was a bit too much to handle. "I was thinking I could go to the hotels to see if she's been recently hired on in any type of maid or server role."

"That's one option," Helena agreed, although the furrow was back in her brow. "But I was thinking of using Luna to help track Zoe, see if my partner can pick up her scent. I guess I could do that near the hotels. It might be a way to narrow our focus."

He was forced to admit her plan had merit. "Okay, that's a good idea." He filled two plates with eggs and toast then carried them over to the table. "The only other thought I had was to call Norbert again."

"Your informant?" Helena looked intrigued by the idea. She poured two mugs of coffee and joined him at the table. "Can't hurt, although I'm not convinced he's as honest as you believe him to be."

"I never said he was totally honest," Everett retorted. "No informant is. But he did have information that only a handful of people knew about."

"I guess." Helena clasped her hands together and bowed her head. He felt himself stiffen as she prayed. "Dear Lord, we thank You for this food we are about to eat. We ask that You keep us all safe in Your care, Amen."

Everett couldn't bring himself to meet her gaze.

They both dug into their meals without saying much. He wondered once again how they'd work the case with Christine to care for. If not for the recent brush with danger, they could take her along. There was an infant carry pack in the pink diaper bag they could use just for that purpose.

But considering the recent gunfire that had targeted him and Helena, the backpack wasn't an option.

"I think it might be best if you stay here with Christine while I take Luna to the hotels," Helena said. "I know that won't sit well with you, but once I narrow the search field, it will be easier for you to take Zoe's photo to ask who might have seen her."

He ground his teeth together, then relaxed his jaw with an effort. "You're right, I don't like it. Why don't we just find a babysitter?"

She arched a brow. "Like who?"

"I don't know," he admitted. "I want the baby to be safe. If we were in Anchorage, it would be easier to find someone to watch her."

"I don't think we have that option in Denali," Helena said. "But we can make some calls. In the meantime, reach out to your contact while I make a quick trip to the hotel. The more information we get, the more likely we are to find Zoe."

She was right. He didn't like it, but he knew it was the best plan. "Okay, fine." He pulled out his cell phone and set it on the table. "But give me your number, and take mine down, too. I want you to call if you need anything."

"Good idea." Helena took out her phone. After they exchanged numbers and programmed them into their respective devices, she took a sip of her coffee. "You really think the hotels are the target?"

"Yes." He spread his hands. "What else is there out here? Besides, the new hotel is having a grand opening in a few days. That would be the perfect opportunity for the crime ring to strike."

"I guess." Her gaze was troubled. "I hate thinking that Zoe might still be with those crooks. I'm hoping she left Christine with us so she could disappear for a while."

He didn't think that was the plan at all, but wisely held his tongue. He needed Helena to keep working with him on this, not against him. "Why don't you start by taking Luna to the new hotel? If you don't find Zoe's scent there, then you can move on."

"I can do that," Helena agreed. Luna padded over to nudge the baby who was kicking her legs with exuberance. "Christine looks like she wants to be out of that seat."

That gave him an idea. "Let's drove together to the new hotel. We'll wear our respective uniforms, to indicate we're doing police business. I'll stay in the car with Christine, while you and Luna head out to do your tracking thing."

"Do you think it's safe?" Helena asked.

"I think it's safer for us to be together, than apart."

After they made quick work of washing their dishes and cleaning up the kitchen, Everett headed off to shower and change into his uniform.

When he stepped into the living room, he was relieved to see that Helena was wearing hers, as well. Although, it was still a bit wrinkled from being drenched in the rain and she didn't have her hat. He inwardly groaned when he realized he'd left it behind.

Christine was babbling happily by the time he tucked her into the back seat of Helena's SUV.

"You drive," Helena suggested, putting Luna in the rear. He noticed she had the red scarf in a plastic bag clipped to her belt and that Luna was wearing her familiar K-9 vest.

"Fine with me."

The new hotel wasn't too far. The trip took longer, though, because of the lumbering buses slowly making their way around the curvy Denali Park Road.

Everett finally pulled into the parking lot of the Denali Grand Chalet. The hotel was huge and looked like it catered to the super rich, which was interesting considering Denali was a national park. But the owner of the hotel was a billionaire who had lots of rich friends, so maybe it would work.

Anything that offered a financial boon to the State of Alaska was good for everyone who lived there. He glanced at Helena. "I'd feel better if I could back you up. I know your dog is trained to pick up scents, but that won't help protect you against gunfire."

"You are backing me up by being in the SUV. I'll signal or call if anything happens." Helena didn't wait for his response but pushed out of the vehicle and went around to release Luna.

From the driver's seat, he watched as she offered the scent bag to the animal before giving Luna the command to seek.

The dog lifted her nose, searching for the familiar scent. As they took off, he noticed the animal didn't travel in a straight line. Instead,

Luna zigzagged a path around the parking lot and toward the front door.

He wondered if they should have started at one of the side entrances, a more likely spot for employees to come and go. But Zoe would have had to come in through the main entrance to apply for a job, wouldn't she?

How long did a human scent linger in an area, anyway?

He had no clue.

He divided his attention between watching Helena and Luna, and eyeing Christine in the rearview mirror. The baby was content to play with her rattle, shaking it every which way.

When he noticed Helena and Luna heading around the hotel to one of the side entrances, he put the SUV in gear and moved to a new parking space to continue watching over them.

Tracking Zoe's scent seemed to be taking a while, which he had to assume wasn't a good sign. He drummed his fingers on the steering wheel, wondering what the target was if not a new hotel that catered to the rich.

Unless Zoe wasn't working for the hotel, but some sort of contract company? Normally, hotels had their own kitchen and service staff, but maybe the owner hadn't been able to hire enough locals to do the job.

Everett knew for certain that Zoe had worked

for a catering company on one job and had also worked as a hotel maid during the anniversary gathering.

But no matter how hard he'd tried, he hadn't been able to come up with a connection between all the thefts and one single contract company.

He caught a glimpse of Helena praising Luna. He straightened in his seat as she led the K-9 back to the SUV.

"She found Zoe's scent near the employee entrance," Helena said breathlessly. "That means she's been here recently."

"That's excellent work, Helena." He had to stop himself from embracing her. Instead, he focused his gaze on the large hotel. Now that they knew Zoe worked there in some sort of capacity, they could focus their attention on finding her.

And hopefully convince her to testify against the others in the criminal ring while keeping her out of danger.

SIX

Helena stared at the large hotel through the windshield of the SUV. Zoe had recently been near the employee entrance. But did that mean she actually worked for the hotel? Or that she'd escaped from it?

She had no way of knowing for sure.

"This time, it's your turn to stay here while I go inside to see if Zoe is an employee," Everett said, breaking into her thoughts.

"Okay, but they may not share employee information without a warrant," she warned.

"I know, and I can probably get one, but that would mean heading back to Anchorage to take the paperwork to the judge." He shrugged. "I can ask one of my fellow officers to do that for me, but that will still take time. In the interim, I'll see if they're willing to cooperate."

"Anything is possible." She glanced back at Christine, who was happily gnawing on a rattle ring with plastic keys. "I'm sure we'll be fine."

Sitting in the SUV with the engine running to keep the interior cool for Christine and Luna, Helena kept a keen gaze on the people coming and going in the hotel, hoping to catch a glimpse of Zoe.

The minutes dragged by. Suddenly she saw a man step out from the employee entrance, then slink around the back of the building. Helena quickly put the SUV in gear and drove over to get a better look. But there was no sign of him.

Frustrated, she returned to her original parking spot. When Christine began to fuss, she turned in her seat and unbuckled the little girl. The baby smiled and waved her arms, gazing around with curiosity.

She held Christine up so that her feet were pressed on her legs. The baby seemed to enjoy these moments of freedom, and Helena once again found it incredible that Zoe had given birth without telling her.

Had the baby's father been in the delivery room with her? Or had her twin been all alone? Her heart squeezed in her chest at the thought of Zoe going through something like that without any support.

When Everett returned, his expression was grim. "They wouldn't give me the information. I showed Zoe's picture to a few of the employees I ran across, and they all claimed they didn't know her."

Helena sighed softly, still bouncing Christine on her lap. "Let's head back to the cabin, so you can get the paperwork started for a warrant, and maybe we'll learn something from your contact, too."

"Yeah." Everett scowled. "I told them Zoe might be in danger, but even that didn't make them budge."

She held Christine with one arm and rested her other hand on Everett's forearm. "Remember, there are privacy laws they're being held to, and breaking them opens the hotel management to litigation."

"I know, it's just frustrating." He sighed and reached for the baby. "Let's get her into her car seat so we can head back to the cabin."

Helena relinquished Christine but was loathe to leave the hotel where Luna had captured Zoe's scent. It was the closest they'd come to finding her twin, even though she knew that Zoe could be long gone by now.

As if reading her mind, Everett said, "Don't worry, we'll be back once we get the warrant."

"I know." She hesitated then added, "I saw a guy come out of the employee entrance and disappear behind the building. But when I drove over there, he was gone. I'd like to see if Luna can pick up Zoe's trail leading away from the hotel. It might give us a clue as to where she's staying."

Everett nodded slowly. "It's worth a try."

Eager to be doing something constructive to track her twin, Helena slid out of the vehicle again and freed Luna from the rear. She took Luna back over to the hotel's employee entrance and then offered the scarf again.

"Seek, Luna. Seek Zoe!"

Luna wagged her fluffy tail and went to work, putting her nose to the ground. As before, she alerted near the doorway. Helena praised her K-9 partner, gave her a treat, then issued the command again.

"Seek Zoe."

Eager to please, Luna sniffed along the ground. She made a crisscross pattern, widening her search zone. The K-9 alerted near a parking space roughly twenty feet from the doorway.

"Good girl!" Helena rubbed her hands over Luna's furry coat and offered another treat. "You're a good girl! Seek Zoe!"

Luna wagged her tail and returned to sniffing, but ended up right back at the employee entrance, alerting there once again.

"Good girl!" Helena gave her partner more

positive reinforcement, but deep down, she felt dejected.

The trail ended in the parking lot.

Everett had pulled up near the parking spot, so it didn't take her long to settle Luna in the SUV. "I take it, the trail stops here?"

"Yeah." She grimaced. "I guess the only good news about that is that we know someone in the crime ring has a vehicle of some sort. The driver must have dropped her off and picked her up, parking in this spot." She waved her hand at the area where Luna had alerted. "But that also means we are no closer to finding where she's staying now."

"It's more than we knew before," Everett pointed out. "And plays into my idea of this hotel being the next target."

She nodded but didn't say anything.

Everett circled the parking lot and pulled back onto the highway, still laden with several large tour buses.

Her K-9 partner had an incredible nose for tracking scents, so really all they knew for certain was that Zoe had been there within the past couple of days. Luna could track scents in the rain, but considering the massive thunderstorm they'd experienced, Helena still felt certain that Zoe had been at the hotel recently.

Had her twin gone into hiding after dropping

off Christine at Everett's cabin? The way Luna had lost the scent near the highway made her doubt that theory. Someone had picked Zoe up at the side of the road.

Friend or foe? Could her sister have found someone willing to help her? The way Helena had been attacked and later, how a gunman had sneaked up on her at Everett's cabin, made that seem unlikely.

No, the more she thought about it, the more likely it was that Zoe was still in danger. Maybe even from Christine's father.

She sent up a quick prayer to ask God to keep Zoe safe in His care.

Everett felt waves of tension radiating from Helena and knew she was stressing about her twin.

As much as he still believed Zoe was guilty of grand theft, he was beginning to see how she might have been forced into cooperating with the guy in charge of the criminal ring.

Especially if that same guy was Christine's father.

In his humble opinion, Zoe should have turned herself in. Yet, having a baby, especially if the guy in charge really was Christine's father, may have made that difficult.

Although, now that the baby was safe, shouldn't Zoe be able to find a way to escape?

Or did the woman intend on sticking with her man, regardless of the crimes they'd committed? It was possible that Zoe intended to continue in her life of crime.

He didn't dare voice his thoughts out loud, knowing Helena would immediately reject the idea. But it was something he needed to consider.

After getting off the park road, which again took much longer than it should have thanks to the slow-moving tour buses, he made several turns and backtracked to be sure they hadn't been followed. When he finally deemed it safe, Everett returned to the cabin.

He carried Christine and her infant seat inside, while Helena took care of Luna. As they entered the cabin, he couldn't help but notice the domesticated scene.

A casual observer seeing them together would assume they were a family, complete with a pet dog that looked more like a wolf.

Only they weren't. He'd lost his family and could never replace them.

Never.

After making a quick sweep of the place, to make sure nothing had been disturbed, he set Christine in the center of the room, in a spot where she could see everything going on around her. He pulled out his phone and contacted one of the officers in Anchorage that he trusted implicitly to get what he needed done.

"Trent? I need a favor."

His fellow officer groaned. "Let me guess, you need a search warrant."

Everett couldn't help but smile. "Yep."

"You know, I'm a good cop," Trent argued. "Doing paperwork isn't my only skill. Maybe if you took the time to write up your own requests, you'd get better at it."

"Never said you weren't a good cop," Everett said in a soothing tone. "And you know very well that normally I wouldn't mind doing my own scut work. However, I happen to be in Denali at the moment and could use your help with this one."

"Denali?" Trent sighed loudly. "Okay, fine. Give me the details."

He quickly filled the other officer in on everything he'd gleaned so far.

"That's all you have?" Trent asked when he had finished. "It's pretty thin, Everett. A dog tracking Zoe Maddox's scent outside the employee entrance of the Denali Grand Chalet, and a petty criminal informant providing eyewitness testimony of her handing off expensive jewelry to a man in a baseball cap? Not sure that's enough to convince a judge that she works for the hotel."

"It should be enough," Everett shot back. "Seriously, how else am I supposed to crack this crime ring open?"

"Do you have any other intel that puts her at the hotel?" Trent asked.

"No." He glanced at Christine, who was babbling at Luna sitting protectively beside her. "I can put Zoe in Denali without the dog detecting her scent, but not at that specific hotel." Even that was a bit of a stretch as he couldn't say with one-hundred-percent certainty that Zoe had dropped off Christine. Sure, Luna was a highly trained K-9 with a great track record, but he knew judges often wanted more.

Besides, as much as he wanted that warrant, he had no desire to have to explain about Christine.

At least, not yet.

"I'll do my best, but no promises," Trent said in a grudging tone.

"I appreciate that, thanks." Everett disconnected from the call before the other man could continue to argue.

"Sounds like that warrant isn't a slam dunk," Helena observed.

"It's not." He stared down at his phone. "I'll

contact my informant to see if he can shed any more light on the new hotel being the next target."

Having memorized Norbert's number and hoping the guy hadn't gotten himself a new disposable phone, he quickly made the call. Norbert didn't answer, so he left a message asking him to get in touch with him ASAP.

"You really think he'll call back?" Helena's tone was filled with doubt.

"I hope so." Everett didn't like having their investigation being partially in the hands of a small-time crook, but what else could he do?

Every instinct he possessed told him Zoe was still in Denali.

"So now what?" Helena's forehead puckered with a frown, and he felt certain she was still dealing with the headache from being attacked. Oddly, he wanted to smooth them away.

"I'm running out of ideas," Everett admitted gruffly. "I could flash her picture around some more, but I didn't get the sense anyone was interested in cooperating with me. We can try staking out the hotel to see if we can catch Zoe going in or out."

Christine began to wail, and Luna began to whimper, as if not liking the sound of the baby being upset. With a start, Everett realized it was close to lunchtime.

"I'll get her bottle ready," Helena offered. "I need to get used to the routine."

He nodded and picked up Christine. Luna followed as he paced the interior of the cabin, jostling the infant in his arms. When Helena had the bottle ready, she sat in a chair and held her arms out for the little girl.

Again, the scene was far too familiar. Images of Sheila and Colin flashed in his mind, a deep ache stabbing his heart.

He couldn't take much more of this cozy togetherness.

His fingers curled into helpless fists. He needed to get out. To leave Christine with Helena and head off to solve the case.

Luna nudged his hand with her nose and licked his wrist as if asking to be petted. He let out a silent sigh and glanced down at the animal, reaching to bury his fingers in her thick pelt.

It all came back to working with Helena and Luna. They provided the best chance at finding Zoe.

And once he'd found her, he felt certain she'd provide the name of the guy in charge. She'd only have two choices: tell them what they needed to find and arrest him, or go to jail.

Factoring the baby into the picture, he figured Zoe would do whatever was necessary to stay out of jail.

His cell phone rang, interrupting his thoughts. He recognized Norbert's number. "Thanks for returning my call," he said.

"I told you everything I know," the man whined.

"You've always been great at keeping your ear to the ground, Norbert. I'm sure you must have heard something about the next high-dollar target."

His informant was silent for a long minute. "I mighta heard something about a hotel in Denali."

Everett tightened his grip on the phone. "Which one?"

"The new one. But I can't be sure," Norbert hedged. "I overheard it at the bar last night."

"Anything else? I need more, man, and you know I'm good for it."

"I can't tell you what I don't know." His voice dropped to a whisper. "Gotta go."

There was nothing but dead air on the line.

After calling Trent and giving the added information for the search warrant, Everett turned toward Helena. She was burping Christine like an old pro.

"I'm going to head back to the hotel, keep an eye on things for a while."

"If you're going, we're *all* going." Helena narrowed her gaze. "We're working this as a team, remember?"

"Yeah, okay." He didn't like it, but also didn't like the idea of leaving them here alone.

The thought of anything happening to either of them made him feel sick to his stomach.

"Maybe we should grab something to eat first," he suggested. "Christine should be ready for a nap soon. Her sleeping for a couple of hours would make things easier on us."

"Fine with me."

They ate grilled ham-and-cheese sandwiches and discussed how to best approach the stakeout.

"Being in a police SUV isn't exactly being undercover," Helena pointed out.

"I know, but we can park the SUV in the brush, maybe muddy up the sides a bit and use binoculars."

She nodded. "Okay, it's a plan."

He glanced at Christine, who was still stubbornly wide awake. "Can't say I've ever gone on a stakeout with a baby before."

Helena let out a choked laugh. "Me, either."

They shared a smile and, for a moment, he felt almost...*happy*.

Then Luna began to growl. A deep, rumbling sound that made every instinct flash red alert.

Everett jumped up, his weapon already in hand. "Get Christina and keep her safe."

For once Helena didn't argue. She called Luna to her side while reaching for the infant carrier. In seconds, she took the baby into the back bedroom.

Luna's growling never let up. Everett couldn't believe their location had been compromised once again. Had the noise he'd heard been something more? Maybe, but Luna hadn't scented anything, either. Thankfully, the daylight made it difficult for the bad guys to hide. But that same light worked against him, too.

Everett crept up to the window, scanning the area around the front of the cabin.

"See anything?" Helena called softly.

"Negative."

"We should make a run for it."

He hesitated, torn by indecision. Stay or go? Their compromised location meant they'd need to get away sooner or later.

"Okay, but let me go first."

There was a momentary pause and suddenly Helena was beside him, still holding on to the infant carrier. "I'll back you up. Be careful."

He hated the idea of the baby being in danger. "If I draw gunfire, I'll take off, see if they'll follow me. That way you can get Christine in the vehicle and get out of here."

She didn't answer, but he knew keeping the baby safe would be her top priority.

He opened the door of the cabin just a crack and waited.

Nothing.

Still, Luna's low growls were impossible to ignore. He slid out through the opening and ran in a crouch to the edge of the vehicle.

Still nothing.

A blur of motion caught the corner of his eye. He called out, "Stop, police!"

More silence.

He opened the back door of the SUV and the rear hatch for Luna, and then ran around to the driver's side. Instantly, Helena was there, buckling Christine into the seat while the dog gracefully jumped into the back.

In mere seconds they were barreling down the rutted driveway, leaving the cabin in the dust.

Just when he thought they were in the clear, he heard the crack of a rifle.

The metallic ping as the bullet hit the vehicle made his heart stop.

"Hurry!" Helena urged.

He pressed harder on the gas, sparing a quick glance at the baby through the rearview mirror.

For the first time since losing Sheila and Colin, he prayed.

Please don't take another innocent life, Lord. Not another innocent life.

Would his prayers be answered?

SEVEN

Someone was shooting at them!

"Is the baby okay?" Everett asked, his voice hoarse.

"I think so." Helena gripped the door handle as Everett increased their speed, her mind whirling. Who was out there? The same shooter with a rifle who'd taken a shot at her on the grassy knoll? If so, how had they been found? Only a handful of people knew about their relocation and she trusted Colonel Gallo and the rest of the K-9 team with her life.

She glanced back at the baby, relieved to find Christine's eyes drifting shut. "She's falling asleep."

"Good." Tension radiated from Everett as he focused on the highway.

A heavy silence fell between them. After the first couple of gunshots, one that had pinged the SUV, she hadn't heard any more once they'd reached the highway. That made her wonder if the guy had been in a stationary spot, high up in a tree.

But someone had also been outside the cabin, it was likely what had caught Luna's attention. Her K-9 was good but couldn't track someone way up off the ground in a tree somewhere.

Two bad guys, likely from the criminal ring Zoe had gotten herself entangled with. Were they working together? It was the only explanation she could come up with.

"We need a new place to stay," Helena said as Everett continued to put distance between them and the shooters. "Any ideas?"

Everett's mouth was a grim line. "This would be easier if it wasn't the height of the tourist season."

"I know." She sighed. "I'll call my boss again, see what else she can come up with."

Everett grimaced and nodded. "Okay, but I think it might be better for you and Christine to head back to Anchorage."

"Not happening." She squelched a flash of guilt over keeping the baby with them. "Zoe is here in Denali, and Luna is our best chance of finding her."

He didn't respond, but she could tell by the reluctant acceptance in his gaze that he knew she was right. It was the main reason they'd teamed up to work the case together in the first place.

He didn't like it and, frankly, neither did she. It was never a good idea to expose Christine to danger.

But what was the alternative? The criminal ring was *his* investigation, and he planned to see it through to the end. And so did she.

"We'll both stay the course. Once we find Zoe, I'm sure we'll get the information we need to break the case wide open."

"You *hope* that's what will happen," Helena corrected. "But she could be just an innocent pawn in all of this and may not have as much information as you think."

"Maybe." Everett glanced up at the rearview mirror and she knew he was eyeing the sleeping baby. "But I still believe Christine's father is involved."

She was forced to concede he had a good point. Why else would Zoe go along with all this? Maybe the father was threatening to harm Christine, which is why her twin had taken the risk of dropping off her daughter at Everett's cabin.

Pulling out her phone, she dialed her boss. "This is Helena, our safe house was compromised."

"That's not good news." Helena could imagine the deep frown etching Lorenza's brow. "You haven't even been there twenty-four hours."

"Tell me about it." She didn't want to mention how Everett had called his informant, which may have led to their discovery. "Can you help us find something else?"

"I'll see what I can do. Give me thirty minutes."

She disconnected from the call. "If Lorenza comes up empty, we could try the park rangers. They may know of a place we can use."

"I'd rather keep those who know about our location to a minimum," Everett said. "I already feel guilty enough that we were found."

"We don't know for sure the call to your informant was the leak," she pointed out. "Anchorage is over four hours away. There wasn't enough time for anyone to drive up from there to get to the cabin."

"We know the shooters are here in Denali, and this isn't the first attack on us." He glanced at her. "They might have tapped his phone."

"You think they have that kind of sophisticated technology?" Helena wasn't entirely convinced. "I mean, it's possible, but that means they have access to big-time resources. More so than what we originally believed."

"Possible organized crime connections," Everett murmured. "The way they've eluded capture so far has me leaning in that direction." He hesitated and added, "Don't forget we included the rangers in on this. One of them may be on the take."

The idea of Zoe being linked to organized crime made her stomach knot. And the possibility of the park rangers being involved, wasn't any better. "I hope that's not true, Everett."

"I know." His gaze was grim.

Helena's phone rang, her boss's name on the screen. "Colonel? Did you find something?"

"I did. But try to stay safe here, okay? I'm running out of favors to call in."

"We will." She put the phone on speaker and pulled up the note-taking app. "What's the address?"

As Lorenza relayed the information, she tapped it into her phone, then read it back.

"That's correct. Oh, and there's a punch-code lockbox on the door containing the key. The place is for sale, but the owner has been renting it out. And, as luck would have it, the previous tenant ended up leaving early, so the place is yours for the rest of the month."

"Great, thanks." Helena disconnected and put the address into the GPS. "Turn right at the next intersection," she said. "Looks like this cabin is actually closer to the hotels."

"Good news for us." Everett took the turn. "I still think staking out the Denali Grand Chalet is our best chance of finding Zoe."

"Maybe." If Zoe was, in fact, working there. Could be that she'd tried to get a job but wasn't hired.

Or it could be that her twin was there but had already moved on to something else.

Helena told herself not to focus on the worst-case scenario. Her twin was okay, and she prayed they'd find her before she managed to bury herself deeper into trouble.

"We need more information on the Chalet itself," Everett said as he followed the GPS directions to their new location. "I heard the place was built by some rich guy."

She performed a search on her phone. "It's owned by a billionaire by the name of Jayson Porter. Apparently he's some tech giant CEO and has connections with the Hollywood jet set. His girlfriend is some big actress."

"Great. Talk about the perfect target for someone looking to score." Everett scowled.

"You think so? Wouldn't a billionaire have extensive security? I mean, someone a little less rich and famous might be easier to steal from."

"Not if it's an inside job."

She grimaced. "And you think Zoe is the insider who is tasked with stealing the goods?"

"I think it's a strong possibility." Everett leaned forward. "Is that the driveway there?"

"Yes." The drive leading to the cabin was rutted worse than their previous location. As they approached the safe house, she tried not to wrinkle her nose with distaste. The place didn't look nearly as nice as the previous one.

No wonder it was still on the market.

Everett parked in front of the cabin. She got out and quickly released the dog from the back. "Will you get Christine? I want to walk Luna around the property."

"Sure." Everett was already pulling the infant carrier from the back seat. He gazed down at Christine for a moment then carried her up to the front door. It didn't take him long to punch in the code and open the cabin door.

Helena released the dog. "Come Luna."

The K-9 was all business as they walked around the property. The terrain was more rugged, the thick weeds and brush making it difficult to navigate.

A deterrent for the bad guys who kept finding them? She could only hope. Luna didn't growl or alert on Zoe's scent, not that she expected the dog to find her sister here. When she was satisfied that the property was secure and relatively well hidden from the road, she turned back.

The interior of the cabin left much to be desired, but she knew it could have been worse. "I have a pair of binoculars in the vehicle, do we want to watch the Chalet in shifts? I can do the first one, and you can relieve me after a few hours."

Everett hesitated. "We need to wait a bit on that idea. I still can't figure out how our last location was discovered."

"You don't think Norbert's phone was tapped?"

"If the guy in charge suspected Norbert was talking to me, I think they'd find a way to silence him. I can't help but wonder if we were somehow followed from the Chalet."

"I didn't see anyone behind us, did you?"

"No, although we did pass that park ranger." His expression was grim. "Still, even if the rangers aren't involved, it doesn't mean the bad guys didn't find a way to track us. Especially from a spot high up in the trees. The gunfire was from a rifle, just like the shot taken at you the first day on the hill."

She shivered. If Everett was right about a spotter nestled in a high place with eyes on the Chalet, then they need to rethink their approach.

Unfortunately, she had no idea what their next move should be.

* * *

The baby stirred and began to fuss. Everett picked Christine up from her infant carrier and briefly rested his cheek against her downy head.

When the bullet had hit the vehicle, he'd thought the worst.

"You're okay, little girl," he whispered. "Everything is going to be all right."

The baby quieted in his arms. For a moment, he could barely breathe, the sweetness of the baby hitting him hard.

When Helena and Luna entered the cabin, he felt her curious gaze. "She okay?" she asked.

"Yeah." He reached for the diaper bag. "Christine probably needs to be changed."

"I can do it," Helena offered. "I could use the practice."

Diaper changing wasn't high on his list of fun things to do, but oddly enough it was difficult to hand the baby over. His gaze caught Helena's, and a tingle of awareness rippled over him. He cleared his throat. "You'll do fine."

Helena snuggled the infant and carried her into one of the bedrooms. Meanwhile, he headed into the kitchen, taking note of the lack of food. They'd been forced to leave their previous cabin in too much of a hurry to pack the cooler.

At least Christine had plenty of formula. Zoe had left more than enough for the little girl.

He made a fresh bottle and tried to think of the closest place to grab something to eat. If he could convince Helena to stay here with Luna and Christine, he could run to one of the small grocery stores.

"All changed," Helena announced, carrying her niece into the living room. "But she seems a bit cranky."

"I made a bottle for her. I'm sure she's hungry." He gestured toward the rocking chair. "Have a seat."

Helena sat and accepted the bottle. "You're always one step ahead, aren't you?"

"Not always." He shifted his weight from one foot to the other. "We don't have anything to eat for dinner, so I'm going to head out to pick up some groceries."

"Shouldn't you wait until we can all go together?"

"I'd rather you stay here with the baby, just in case the SUV is a target. The shooter might know the license plate. Besides, I'm confident Luna will guard you."

She frowned then reluctantly nodded. "Okay, but if you're not back in thirty minutes, I'll calling the park rangers to put out a BOLO for you."

That made him smile. "Deal." He still had the keys to the SUV, so he headed outside, glad for something constructive to do.

He parked in front of a small convenience store, pulled out his phone and called the ranger station. "This is Officer Brand, any hits yet on the cigarette butt I dropped off yesterday?"

"Not yet," Ranger Jeff Langley said.

"Any chance you can put a rush on it?" Everett asked. "I know you're busy, but it's important."

"They're all important," Langley grumbled. "And yours isn't the only case we have. All our evidence goes to the crime lab in Anchorage, and it looks like yours went out right after we checked it in. We should have results soon, but I can give them a call."

His lack of enthusiasm made Everett grind his teeth. But he kept his tone genial. "Thanks, I really appreciate it."

After disconnecting the call, he headed inside the store. He'd only pick up the bare necessities, since there was no guarantee they wouldn't be forced back on the run.

It still bugged him that their previous safe house had been found so quickly. And despite his concern over Norbert being compromised, he really didn't think his informant had been the source. Anchorage was four hours away, and these attacks were coming quick.

Not knowing where the danger was coming from was more frightening than anything.

When he had the groceries stored in the SUV, he took another circular route back to the cabin. This time, he looked not just for a tail on the road behind him, but for any sign of a flash of sunlight glinting off glass, indicating a shooter might be hiding and watching through binoculars.

Thankfully, there was no sign of anyone lurking around. He desperately wanted to believe they were safe, here. Yet secretly wondered if they'd be safe *anywhere*.

If the guy in charge of the criminal ring knew Everett and Helena were on to him, then it was likely the attacks would continue.

Unless the Denali Grand Chalet was the last big heist?

Nah, if they got away with stealing from a billionaire, what would be the motivation to stop?

Everett returned to the cabin and unloaded the groceries. "I picked up rotisserie chicken for tonight, hope that's okay," he said from the kitchen. "Figured neither of us was in the mood to cook."

Helena rose from where she'd been playing

with Christina to join him. "Great idea," she said. "Thanks."

"Not a problem. I hope your warrant comes through so we can find Zoe."

"What's your plan if Zoe is an employee of the Chalet?" Helena joined him at the table to eat. "Are you going to get her boss to turn her over to us?"

"Yeah, that's exactly what I'd like to do. Safer for everyone involved that way."

They ate their meal in silence, and he suspected Helena was considering his plan.

His cell phone rang. Recognizing the number for the ranger station, he quickly answered. "Brand."

Everett put the call on speaker so Helena could listen in.

"This is Jeff Langley. Believe it or not, they lifted a partial print from the cigarette butt you found."

"Were they able to find a match in CODIS?"

"Yeah, the fingerprint belongs to a Gareth Cantwell. You know him? He has an extensive criminal history, although nothing that popped in the past few years."

Everett locked gazes with Helena. "Yeah, I've heard of him. And you're right, he's done time for armed robbery in the past. Thanks, Langley. You've been a huge help."

"Gareth Cantwell?" Helena echoed once he'd put the phone down. "A known felon?"

"I'm afraid so." He sat back in his seat. Knowing Cantwell was involved in the incidents against them, was huge.

But he still didn't know if he was the guy in charge—or a hired gun sent by someone else to do his dirty work.

EIGHT

Helena pulled up Gareth Cantwell's mug shot on her phone, feeling sick at the possibility he could be Christine's father.

Cantwell was handsome in a daredevil way and she could easily imagine Zoe—who'd always been drawn to the bad boys in town—getting involved without realizing the types of crimes he'd committed.

Until it was too late.

"Christine doesn't look anything like him," she said.

"We don't know what role Cantwell plays in this," Everett cautioned. "He may not be Christine's father, but someone hired to do a job."

"Maybe." Privately, she wasn't convinced. He looked like Zoe's type, down to the tattoo of a skull and crossbones on his right bicep that the mug shot information had noted as an identifying mark. She couldn't seem to tear her gaze away from it.

"Don't, Helena." Everett's voice was soft. "We need to stick with the facts at this point, okay?"

She forced herself to nod. "The fact is, this guy was outside the cabin you'd rented under your name. The same cabin Zoe brought Christine to for safety." That was another reason to believe Gareth Cantwell was Christine's father.

"Yes." Everett stood and came around to look down at the picture on her phone. "I don't remember seeing the tattoo, but he was wearing a long-sleeved jacket. And once he took a shot at me, I hit the ground."

Remembering how close Everett had come to being hit by gunfire made her shiver. "You did the best you could."

"I guess. Things happened pretty fast." He scowled at the image. "But I'm fairly certain Cantwell was the shooter I chased off."

"That's more than we knew an hour ago." Helena tried to think positive. "When we get the warrant for the HR records, we can look for Cantwell's name, too."

"As a felon, he wouldn't pass the background check." Everett stacked their dirty plates and carried them to the sink. "But Zoe would."

Yes, her sister would pass a background check. Her parents had always bailed Zoe out of trouble. Until they'd moved to Arizona to retire. Leaving Zoe to fend for herself. And Helena refusing to take up their bailing-out role, telling her twin to be responsible for her own actions.

Had she been too hard on Zoe after their parents' move? Had she pushed her twin over the edge, so that she'd felt her only recourse was to join forces with Cantwell?

Helena felt certain the answer was a resounding yes.

Christine's cry caught her attention. Turning toward the infant carrier, she smiled when Luna gently nudged the baby with her nose. Christine offered a toothless grin and reached out to grab a handful of Luna's silver-gray fur.

"Your K-9 is very protective of her, isn't she?" Everett was watching the interaction, too. "I think she'd rip apart anyone who tried to harm the baby. I never realized how much a dog can contribute to law enforcement activities."

"Yes. Luna, in particular as a Norwegian elkhound, has good tracking and suspect apprehension abilities, in addition to being extremely protective."

"I can see that." Everett leaned against the counter and crossed his arms over his chest. "One thing I still don't understand is why Cantwell came to the cabin in the first place. If that first shot at you was a warning, he'd know about the K-9 and had to realize we out-numbered him."

"It's been bothering me, too. Not just that first attack, but all of them. It doesn't seem to be a good use of their time to keep coming after us."

Everett's gaze turned thoughtful. "Maybe they think they'll be in the clear if they take us out of the equation."

"But murdering two cops would bring all kinds of law enforcement down on their heads," she countered. "Bringing way more focus on whatever they have planned at the Grand Chalet."

"True." His brow furrowed. "Or maybe these attacks are just bad enough to make us keep moving, rather than trying to take us out of the picture." He grimaced. "If that's their strategy, it's working."

She glanced again at Christine. Was it possible Cantwell wanted the baby back, to use as leverage against Zoe? Maybe the attacks were his way of proving the baby was still vulnerable if her sister didn't do what he said.

Her phone buzzed. Recognizing the colonel's number, she quickly answered. "Maddox."

"Helena? It's Katie. The colonel wants a staff meeting ASAP. Are you able to participate by video conference?"

"Yes, of course." Katie Kapowski was Lorenza's administrative assistant and was very good at making sure everything ran smoothly. "It's six o'clock in the evening, which is an unusual time for a staff meeting, has something happened?"

There was a momentary hesitation before Katie responded. "I'm not sure. Lorenza said this is an update on recent evidence that's come in related to the missing bride."

"Okay," Helena agreed.

"Shouldn't take long," the other woman assured her. "I've sent everyone a link, join as soon as you can."

"Will do." Helena disconnected from the call and quickly checked her work email for the link. In a few minutes, she could see that several other team members were already on the call.

"Maddox checking in," she said.

"We're just waiting for Will— Oh, there he is now." Lorenza nodded. "Okay, thanks for joining everyone. I wanted everyone to hear the latest on our missing bride. Will and Scout have been following up on the tip identifying Lance Wells and Jared Dennis being seen in Anchorage. Any update on that, Will?"

"Unfortunately, not," Will said, frustration lacing his tone. "We're still searching, though."

"Okay, then," Lorenza said briskly. "Tala, would you provide your update?"

"Sure." Tala Ekho sounded a tad nervous. "I did a DNA check on the gum wrapper found at the Family K Reindeer Sanctuary…" The forensic scientist hesitated before adding, "The DNA indicates there is a family connection."

"Impossible," Katie interjected loudly in an unusual outburst. Normally, she was there to take notes, but since her aunt owned the reindeer sanctuary located a few miles outside Anchorage, this new development clearly impacted her on a personal level. "My only living relative is Aunt Addie, there is no one else."

"I understand this is upsetting news," Lorenza said, "but DNA doesn't lie. There could be some long-lost cousin of yours out there somewhere."

"But—Aunt Addie wouldn't lie about that!" There was a hint of desperation in Katie's tone. "Maybe Tala made a mistake?"

"I checked the results twice," Tala offered, not taking offense at having her skills questioned.

"Try not to overthink this, Katie. Could be your aunt doesn't know anything about the family member," Lorenza said soothingly. "At this point, we need to stick to the facts."

Good advice. Exactly what Everett had said to Helena earlier.

Katie fell silent, but Helena sensed the assistant still didn't believe the DNA results.

"Where's Brayden?" Hunter McCord asked. "I just noticed he's the only team member not on the video call."

Brayden Ford, another K-9 Unit member, was paired up with Ella, a female Newfoundland that specialized in underwater search and rescue.

"Brayden is currently off the grid—deep in Chugach State Park, following up on a lead related to the Seavers," Lorenza said. Helena knew the Seavers were a survivalist family who preferred to stay off grid. "We're doing this to help Eli. His godmother is very sick and Eli is desperate to visit her."

"Did Brayden find the Seavers there?" Helena asked.

"There's evidence they were at the location, but they must have gotten a tip that we were out looking for them, because they disappeared without a trace." Lorenza sounded dejected and Helena knew that when one member of the team was hurting, they all felt it. "Helena, what have you found related to your missing sister?"

She quickly explained about the multiple attacks, forcing them to move locations, along with the scant bits of evidence they'd found. "We're waiting for a search warrant to be approved to see if Zoe might be employed at the new Denali Grand Chalet hotel, as they're having a big-splash grand opening event on Friday."

"Good idea, please keep us posted on any new developments," Lorenza said. "And call if you need backup."

"Will do," Helena assured her. The only plan they had so far was to stake out the hotel, and she didn't want to use their precious K-9 resources for the mundane task.

"Anyone else have an update?" Lorenza asked.

There was a long moment of silence.

"Okay, we'll touch base again in a few days. It's important to stay in touch when we're spread thin like this," the colonel added.

There was a chorus of goodbyes, and Helena felt a strange sense of sadness when the call ended. She was close to her teammates and hadn't realized how much she'd missed them.

"Are you okay?" Everett asked.

"Fine." She felt silly for allowing her feelings to show. "Although the progress on the missing bride case is going slower than anticipated."

Everett nodded. "The problem with Alaska is

that it's so big and remote. It's good if you want to hide but makes our job in bringing criminals to justice that much harder."

"True." Helena went over to help wash the dishes. They worked in silence for a moment, her mind drifting back to Gareth Cantwell and the criminal enterprise Zoe had gotten herself mixed up in. "One thing I've been trying to understand is why none of the stolen items has been recovered yet. You'd think they'd need the cash to finance their operation."

"I agree, it's a strange twist. Most criminals are anxious to exchange their loot for cash, but this ring seems determined to keep all the stolen items hidden."

"Hidden where?" Helena glanced at him. "Any ideas?"

"Not a one," he said on a sigh. "Although my gut tells me the goods are either here in Denali or back in Anchorage, as those are the two places we know they're working."

She thought about that for a moment. "The Denali Grand Chalet has been in the news for a while now, which makes me wonder if this target is the grand finale. The plan could be to leave the area to head down to the Lower 48 to fence the goods."

Everett nodded slowly. "I thought the same

thing. If so, then we need to catch them in the act before they have the chance to escape."

"Yes." Helena glanced again at Christine. The idea that Zoe's daughter would grow up without her mother being a part of her life was unacceptable.

They had to find her sister. And soon.

Everett could see the distress on Helena's face and wished there was something he could do to make her feel better. He cared about Helena, more than he should.

But this mess was partially Zoe's doing. Sure, she may have started out innocent enough, but by now there was no way Helena's twin sister didn't know what was going on.

The baby began to fuss, so Helena crossed over to lift her out of the carrier. "Hmm, smells like you need a change."

It was on the tip of his tongue to offer to do the job, but she seemed okay with the task. She rummaged in the pink diaper bag and pulled out the necessary supplies.

Ten minutes later, she brought Christine back and set her in the infant carrier once again. "How can we get more information on Cantwell?" she asked. "Someone must know something about the guy."

"I can try calling my informant, although I'm

leery because of what happened after I called him from the last cabin."

She frowned. "What's the alternative?"

There wasn't a good way around it. "Maybe I should use your phone. Could be a different number will throw them off."

Unless, of course, Norbert was feeding information directly to the criminal enterprise. This was why you didn't trust your informants any further than you could throw them. "Sure, it's worth a shot." Helena handed him her phone.

"Thanks. I'll keep it short." He shrugged. "My main goal is to toss Gareth Cantwell's name out there, see if I get a reaction."

She moved closer as if wanting to listen in, so he once again put the call on speaker. There were several rings before Norbert answered.

"What?"

"Can you talk?" Everett could hear background noise and didn't want to put his informant in a difficult situation.

Norbert muttered a curse. "Hang on." The background noise faded. "Why are you calling from a different number?"

"Because someone is feeding information about my location to guys with guns. You know anything about that?"

"No. Do you think I want anyone to know

I'm talking to you?" his informant demanded. "I have my own hide to worry about."

Everett locked gazes with Helena, silently seeing if she thought he should continue. She nodded.

"Know a guy by the name of Gareth Cantwell?"

There was a very slight pause before Norbert responded. "No, why? Is he involved?"

Without looking into his beady eyes, Everett couldn't be sure Norbert was telling him the truth. That pause made him think the other man had indeed recognized the name.

"If I find out you're holding back information from me, I'll make sure everyone and their brother knows we've been talking," Everett threatened. He didn't really plan to out the guy, but he really needed to know about Cantwell. "I can tell you recognize his name, so stop stalling."

This pause was longer than the first. "Okay, yeah, I recognize the name. But he's way above my pay grade."

Anticipation swelled. "What do you mean by that?"

"He does big jobs, not small ones. You know what I mean?"

Everett was afraid he did. "Do you think he's the guy in charge of the entire operation?"

"Maybe..." Norbert hedged. "He's known to

be ruthless to those who dare to double-cross him, so I have stayed far away from the dude. I don't need that kind of trouble."

The edge of fear in his tone sounded too real to be faked. "Any idea where I can find him?" Everett asked.

"No. Haven't you been listening? I steer clear of guys like Cantwell." Norbert abruptly disconnected from the line.

Clenching his jaw, Everett handed Helena the phone. "We didn't learn much, I'm afraid."

"Other than Gareth Cantwell is bad enough to scare your informant." She spun away, pacing the small interior of the cabin. "I hate knowing Zoe is involved with him."

"I know." He watched her pace, noting Luna's gaze followed her handler's movements. "I'm sorry."

She grimaced. "Not your fault." She dragged a hand through her hair, and her jerky pacing continued. "Maybe we should get his mug shot over to the park ranger station. Their team may have a better chance of running across him than we would."

It wasn't a bad idea. "I'll send the photo via email, and we can also check in with them in the morning."

"Denali is huge, with far too many places

to hide," she continued as if talking to herself. "He could have Zoe anywhere."

Everett wasn't convinced Cantwell was holding Zoe hostage, yet couldn't deny any threat toward Christine may be enough to keep Helena's twin in line. "We'll find him." He injected confidence in his tone.

Helena abruptly stopped pacing and pulled out her phone. He couldn't see who she was calling, but it didn't matter as the call ended as quickly as it started.

"She's still not answering," she said in a low voice. "He must have taken her phone away after she tried to contact me."

Anything was possible, so he wisely held his tongue.

"DNA," she said, turning to him. "We know his fingerprint is a match, but what about his DNA? When can we get those results?"

Everett followed her gaze to Christine. "You want to find out if Cantwell is Christine's father?"

"Yes." The flash of interest in her dark eyes faded. "It doesn't matter, though, does it?"

"No. I mean, we'll find out eventually, but won't get the DNA results before the grand opening." He couldn't stand watching her pace. He crossed over and gently held her slim shoulders with both hands. "Helena, we can't keep thinking about the worst-case scenario in all this. Right now, we need to find Zoe, and Cantwell, preferably before they pull off another big heist right under our noses."

Her body went still, her eyes downcast. "I know you think Zoe is a willing participant in all this, but what if she isn't? He took her phone for a reason. And she went to great lengths to drop Christine off at your cabin."

"True," Everett agreed. As much as he wanted—*needed*—to keep his distance, the fear and worry in her eyes was too much for him to resist. Gently, he pulled her into his embrace. "We'll find your sister, Helena."

"I hope so—" Her voice cracked and then her body began to shake with sobs.

He cradled her close, telling himself she didn't feel perfect in his arms.

Her crying jag didn't last long. Once she pulled herself together, she lifted her head to gaze up at him, a chagrined look on her face. "Sorry to get your shirt wet."

"I'll survive," he said wryly. "I'm more concerned about you."

"Thanks." Their gazes caught and held. Every muscle in his body tensed when his eyes dropped to her mouth. The logical side of his brain told him this was a bad idea, but he ignored the tiny voice, going with his instinct instead.

And when his mouth captured hers, he felt the impact of their kiss all the way to the soles of his feet.

NINE

Helena lost herself in Everett's kiss, reveling in the sensation of being held and cherished in a way that made her heart swell with hope.

It had been so long.

Too long.

But the unexpected kiss was over far too quickly as Everett lifted his head, swallowed hard and took several steps back. "I—shouldn't have done that."

The regret in his gaze made her sad. "No apology necessary, and I appreciate your support. Thinking about Zoe being mixed up with Cantwell…" She shook her head and shrugged. "I know you were just trying to comfort me."

He looked relieved at her words, as if he'd thought she'd expect something more after a mere kiss.

Christine began to fuss, so she turned her attention to the baby. "Must be time for one last bottle before bed."

"I'll do it." Everett was all too eager to get the supplies from the diaper bag and head into the kitchen.

"It's okay, sweetie, your bottle is coming." Luna stayed close as she cuddled Christine, swaying back and forth, the way Everett had done, in an attempt to soothe the baby.

For years, since her fiancé, Kade Jones, had made her choose between him and her career, she'd remained focused on work. Her job was important, critical, really, to the State of Alaska where law enforcement officials were difficult to find. Being a part of the Alaska State Trooper K-9 Unit was a rare opportunity and one she'd cherished.

But looking into Christine's wide eyes, she thought for the first time that she might be missing something in her life.

A family.

Was she crazy to think that Kade might have had a point? Not that he should have made her choose between her career and him, but maybe her job shouldn't be her highest priority.

A family was far more important than any career.

"Here you go." Everett handed her the bottle.

She shifted Christine, settling her into the crook of her arm, and sat on the sofa, offering the nourishment. Luna joined her, sitting at her feet.

The way the infant put her hands up on either side of the bottle, as if to help hold it in place, made Helena smile. "I guess she was really hungry."

Everett tucked his hands in the pockets of his uniform pants and nodded. "And she's sleeping through the night, which is great."

"Don't most babies sleep through the night by this age?" Her knowledge of infants was sorely lacking.

"No." The corner of his mouth tipped up in a crooked smile. "Colin was fussy and didn't sleep through the night hardly at all…" His voice trailed off as his expression turned somber.

She realized Everett's wife and son had been killed before the baby had gotten a chance to do much of anything.

Including sleeping through the night.

She couldn't imagine how difficult it must be to have Christine here in the cabin with them, a constant reminder of what he'd lost.

Although, deep down, she considered that this could be a part of God's master plan. A way to force Everett into moving forward with his life. To show him that it was okay to experience joy while interacting with another baby.

Children were God's gift to the world. It was only right to cherish them.

It was impossible to understand why He had taken Everett's wife and young son. But life did go on, and maybe, just maybe there was still joy and love waiting out there somewhere for Everett.

If he found a way to let go of the guilt he carried with him like a shield, warding off anyone who dared get too close.

Hard to believe he'd actually kissed her. At least, before his brain had gotten involved.

Maybe his shield of guilt was becoming too heavy to keep lugging around. She hoped she'd be there when he set it aside, for good.

"I, um, think we should call it a night," Everett said, breaking the prolonged silence. "We'll plan our stakeout at the Grand Chalet in the morning."

"Okay. But it's possible Zoe is working evenings instead of days if she's really been put in a position to participate in a big theft."

"I thought of that, too," he admitted. "And I'm still hoping we'll get the search warrant by morning, which will make our job much easier."

She nodded then removed the bottle and put the baby up against her shoulder to burp her. "All right, we'll check in on the status of the warrant in the morning." She paused then added softly, "Good night, Everett."

"Good night." Once again their gazes clashed and she thought she saw something—maybe a flash of regret in his eyes?

More likely her imagination playing tricks on her.

When the baby finished eating, eyelids drooping heavily, Helena set the bottle aside and simply stared into Christine's peaceful face, her heart swelling with love.

"We're going to find your mommy," she whispered, trailing the tip of her fingertip down her niece's satiny cheek. "You'll be together again, very soon."

Helena stood and gently set Christine in the infant carrier. The little girl shifted slightly but didn't wake.

"Come, Luna." Helena took the dog outside, to alert for anything out of the ordinary, before bringing her K-9 partner back in.

Helena picked up Christine. Luna followed her into the second bedroom and Helena prayed once again, for God to keep them safe while helping them to find Zoe.

Despite his bone-weary exhaustion, Everett didn't sleep well.

He never should have kissed Helena. Because

now that he had, he couldn't seem to erase the impact of their brief embrace from of his mind.

This weird attraction for Helena had to stop. Right here and right now. He wasn't interested in being involved romantically. With anyone.

So why on earth had he kissed her?

And worse, why did he want to kiss her again?

This enforced togetherness was getting to him. It was a reminder of the family he'd once taken for granted.

The wife and child he'd lost.

The family he'd never have again.

He must have dozed a bit, because Christine's babbling woke him. This sixth sense he had in responding to the baby must be a holdover from those early days with Colin.

Padding into the main cabin, he went straight over to pick up Christine, who looked as if she was ready to cry. Tucking her close, he prepared a new bottle.

"Cool your jets, little lady," he said in a low voice. "No need to wake the others, okay?"

While feeding the baby, he thumbed through his messages with one hand. Nothing from Trent on their warrant.

The day shift didn't start until eight, and it was only six thirty now, so he'd have to wait a bit before calling.

But why was the paperwork taking so long? Normally, a warrant could be turned around within a day, two at the most.

With a wry smile, he realized today was just the second day. With everything that had been going on, it seemed far longer.

"Morning," Helena said with a wide yawn as she and Luna emerged from the bedroom. "Did I sleep through her crying?"

"No, she was just gearing up when I heard her."

"Okay. Come, Luna." Helena led her K-9 outside.

By the time Christine was fed and changed, and they'd had their own breakfast, the hour was close to eight o'clock.

"I need to check on the status of the warrant," he told Helena.

"Okay. I'm going to work with Luna outside for a bit. With everything going on, I haven't spent much time playing with her."

"Playing?" He lifted a brow. Since when was playing with a dog a priority?

"It's a key element of her training," Helena explained. "Dogs respond really well to play time…it's why they're so eager to work."

"Huh. Learned something new today."

After Helena and Luna went outside, he called his buddy Trent. There was no answer, so he left a message, urging the officer to call him back about the search warrant. If this didn't work, they'd have no choice but to go through with the stakeout. No easy task considering they had Christine to care for.

They'd have to find a good spot to hide while keeping watch with binoculars. But even then, the idea of possibly putting Helena and Christine in harm's way didn't sit well with him.

Not when their last two safe houses had ended up compromised.

His phone rang about ten minutes later. His pulse kicked up as he recognized Trent's number. "Tell me you have good news," he said by way of greeting.

"Hello to you, too, Brand." His buddy's tone was dry. "And yes, I have good news. The warrant was just approved. I'm in the process of getting a copy sent over from the courthouse."

"Will you scan it and send it to me? I need to present it to the hotel human resources department."

"Yeah, but give me a few minutes, okay? I've barely finished my first cup of coffee."

"I'm on my third cup, but I've been up since six thirty," Everett replied. "Thanks again, Trent. Really appreciate this."

"Yeah, I know. And it's all for the greater

good of capturing these crooks. Keep an eye on your email, should show up shortly."

Everett ended the call with a feeling of relief. Finally, they had something concrete to go on.

Impatient, he watched his email like a hawk. The warrant finally arrived about fifteen minutes after the call.

"This is it, Christine," he said, waving the phone at her. "We've got what we need to find your mom."

Helena and Luna walked into the cabin a minute later. She quirked her brow at his wide grin. "Looks like you've got good news."

"We have the warrant. Time to head over to the Denali Grand Chalet to get their employee list."

"Wonderful! I'll be ready to go in a couple of minutes."

While he waited, he tucked Christine's things back into the pink diaper bag and emptied the contents of the fridge, as well. Based on the past few days, he wanted to be prepared in case they couldn't get back to the cabin for some reason.

Safer to have everything they could possibly need in the SUV with them, just in case.

Helena emerged from the bathroom wearing her uniform, which surprisingly looked better than it had the day before. "Steam from the shower," she said as if reading his mind. "And at some point, we need to go back and get my hat."

"Sorry about that." He still felt guilty for leaving it behind. "I have Christine's things packed, you might want to grab Luna's dishes, too."

Her expression turned grim. "You're right."

Traveling with a baby and a dog took time and planning, but soon they were settled in the police SUV and on their way down to the Chalet.

"I hope Zoe is working the early shift today," he said, breaking the silence. "We really need a break in this case."

"And Christine needs her mother," Helena said with a hint of sarcasm in her tone.

"I know she does," he hastened to reassure her.

Helena glanced back at the baby but didn't say anything more.

When he pulled up in front of the Chalet, he glanced at her. "You want to stay here with Christine?"

She wrinkled her nose. "Okay, but let me know what you find out as soon as possible."

"I will."

"Oh, and don't talk to Zoe alone if you find her. Have her brought to a conference room so we can all be in there together," Helena added. "I think it's important for her to see Christine."

"Understood." It was a good plan, but first they needed proof that Zoe was even there. "I'll call you as soon as I know when and where she's working."

"Thanks."

Everett slid out from behind the wheel, holding the door open so Helena could switch places. He hoped she wouldn't need to make a quick escape, but anything was possible.

Walking inside the Grand Chalet, he felt as if he'd entered an alternate universe. High cathedral ceilings with fancy chandeliers wasn't exactly what he'd expected for a resort in Denali. Most of the hotels had a more rustic theme, but not this one. There was a lot of glass and chrome, making him wonder about the clientele the owner was trying to attract.

People from outside the state, most likely. Although, in his experience, those who came to visit from the Lower 48 came specifically to experience the great outdoors and to appreciate the natural wildlife.

Whatever, the business plan for the Grand Chalet wasn't his problem. The fact that the hotel reeked of money, made it even more likely this was the next target. There wouldn't be a better place to find a lot of people with jewelry and cash, so why not make this the big event?

His job was to stop it.

He went up to the desk, showed his badge and the warrant and requested to speak with someone in charge of human resources.

Two minutes later, a beautiful woman wearing high heels and a red suit approached him. "I'm Claire Farnsworth, Director of HR."

"Ms. Farnsworth, I'm Officer Everett Brand from the Anchorage PD. I have a warrant here requiring you to release a list of all employees."

She looked annoyed. "I'm sorry, but that's impossible."

"I assure you, it's not." He glanced at the woman behind the check-in desk. "Maybe we can discuss this in private?"

"Fine." The HR director led him down the hall to another glass door leading into an office suite. When they were settled in her office, she glared at him. "I'd like to see that warrant."

"Of course." He lifted his phone. "What's your email address? I'll send it to you."

She curled her lip as if she didn't trust a warrant that came through email but provided her address. He shot it off to her and waited for her to pull it up on her desktop computer screen.

"This is ridiculous," she said. "I don't understand why you need to know the name of every employee working here."

"Ma'am, I'm trying to prevent a criminal attack on this hotel," he said calmly. "I would think that keeping something bad from happening would be in your best interest."

She drummed red-tipped nails on the desktop. "It looks legit," she said slowly. "But I need to show this to my legal team."

"Go ahead." Everett sat back and crossed his arms at his chest. "I'll wait."

The woman looked as if she wanted to argue but picked up the phone and spoke in a low tone. He watched as she forwarded the email to someone else. Finally, she hung up the phone.

"Our lawyer says we have to comply, but it will take me some time to run the report," Ms. Farnsworth said in a grudging tone. "If you wouldn't mind waiting in the lobby, I'll bring it down as soon as it's available."

"Okay, thank you." He rose. "Just make sure every single employee is on that list, including you."

She bristled but didn't respond.

After returning to the lobby, he called Helena. "Had to jump through a legal hoop, but I should have the report in a few minutes."

"Great. Call me back as soon as you find anything out."

"I will." He disconnected from the call and glanced at his watch. He'd give the HR director five minutes.

And she took every one of those five minutes. Just as he was about to head back into the HR office suite, Ms. Farnsworth crossed the lobby, her high-heeled shoes clicking against the tiled floor.

"Here you go, Officer Brand." She thrust a sheaf of papers at him. "They are in alphabetical order."

"Thank you." He quickly scanned the pages, heading to the M's for Maddox.

Nothing. No Zoe Maddox.

With a frown, he checked again, going slower to make sure he hadn't missed it. Then he tried scanning the Z's just to be sure.

"Wait a minute, are you sure you don't have a Zoe Maddox working for you?"

The woman gave him an irritated look. "The name isn't familiar, and if she's not on the list, then she doesn't work for us."

But Luna had found Zoe's scent near the employee entrance. "Does this list include contracted employees?"

"No. We don't have that information. All contracted employees are the responsibility of the company they work for." She actually looked pleased that her employee list wasn't helpful.

"Do you have a list of companies you contract with?" he demanded.

"I do. But your warrant doesn't give you access to that information." She looked down her nose at him. "Have a good day, Officer Brand."

Anger simmering in his gut, he watched her walk away. Their biggest lead had been a bust. Zoe was not an official staff member of the hotel.

But he felt certain she was on staff with a contract company.

Too bad he had no clue how to find her.

TEN

Waiting patiently was not Helena's strong suit. She divided her time between watching for any sign of Zoe heading for the employee entrance and keeping Christine entertained. Yet knowing Zoe was close and could right now be in the hotel cleaning rooms as a hotel maid or serving meals made staying focused impossible.

The anticipation of seeing her twin again after a year apart was overwhelming.

Her gaze narrowed on a tall man wearing black jeans and black T-shirt. The same guy who'd disappeared behind the building yesterday? She couldn't say for sure. He was heading toward the employee entrance, small plastic keycard in hand. She still had the mug shot of Gareth Cantwell on her phone, and this man clearly wasn't him.

But was he part of the criminal ring? For all she knew, several employees could be involved.

She told herself she was letting her imagination run wild, seeing bad guys around every corner. Finding Zoe was the first step, and her sister could give them the names of anyone else involved.

After what seemed like forever, her phone rang. Everett's name flashed on the screen, filling her heart with hope. "Are you setting up a meeting with Zoe?"

"I'm sorry, Helena." Everett's voice held regret. "She's not on the list of current employees."

She dropped her chin to her chest and closed her eyes. "Are you sure?"

"She's not listed under her current name. Listen, I'm on my way back out with the list. Just wanted you to know."

"Thanks." She hung up, her gaze zeroed in on the front entrance. Within minutes, Everett emerged carrying a sheaf of papers in his hand. Shifting her gaze to the employee entrance, she saw another guy approaching, this one much younger and skinnier than the previous man. He also used a keycard to enter the hotel.

Zoe must have a keycard just like it.

Everett slid into the passenger seat, his expression grim. "Do you have any idea if she might use an alias?"

"No. And how would she pass a background check under an alias, anyway?" She took the papers and scanned the names, needing to see for herself that Zoe wasn't listed.

"The HR director confirmed they use some contract staff, but since that wasn't covered under the warrant, wouldn't even share the names of the companies with me." He scowled. "That woman was less than helpful."

Helena folded the paperwork and stuffed it in the console between them. "I guess that means it's stakeout time."

"Yeah." He didn't look enthusiastic about the role. "Let's drive around, see if we can find a place to hide the SUV, which won't be easy since it's clearly labeled as a state trooper vehicle."

Glad to have something constructive to do, Helena put the car in gear and made a wide sweep of the parking lot that stretched all the way around the building.

"What about over there?" She gestured through the steering wheel to a corner of the lot where there were several large trees. "We might be able to squeeze this in between the trees, backing up enough so that it isn't readily visible from other drivers."

"Maybe." Everett leaned forward, peering at the area in question. "That spot does give us a direct line of sight to the employee entrance, but not to the front of the hotel."

"I know, but remember Luna alerted at the employee entrance, not the front. Even if Zoe is an employee with a contract company, I'm sure this is where she'd go in and out of the building."

"Okay, you've convinced me," Everett agreed. "Should we take turns? I don't think we can keep Christine in the car the whole time."

"Yeah, that should work. Do you want to take the first shift? Or should I?" She didn't relish sitting and doing nothing but watching the employee entrance, but sitting in the cabin with Christine wasn't much better.

"I can take it," Everett said. "Let's return to the cabin."

She swung the SUV in a circle, but then hit the brake. "I'd like to have Luna scent the area again, just in case."

He hesitated then nodded. "If you think that will help, sure."

She wasn't sure it would help the investigation but considering that nothing was going well on the case so far, having Luna alert on Zoe's scent once again would reassure her they were on the right track.

Luna gracefully jumped out of the SUV, her tail wagging with excitement, eager to get to work. Helena played with the dog for a few minutes then took out the scent bag.

"Zoe," she said, presenting the scarf to Luna. "This is Zoe. Seek Zoe. Seek!"

The dog sniffed long and hard then lifted her head. Helena had purposely started in the far corner of the parking lot, to see if Zoe had been in that area. Luna did her zigzag sniffing thing, sometimes doubling back before she made her way closer to the hotel.

From there, it didn't take long for her K-9 partner to pick up the scent trail. Luna alerted in the exact same location as last time, the parking spot where she'd theorized that Zoe had been dropped off, maybe even by Gareth Cantwell, for work.

"Good girl, Luna. You're such a good girl." She praised her K-9 for several moments then said, "Seek. Seek Zoe!"

Once again, Luna followed the trail to the employee entrance and alerted. She praised her some more, feeling relieved.

Luna's nose was great, but scents could fade over time, especially since there were lots of employees who came and went through this doorway. The fact that the K-9 could still track Zoe meant it was highly likely her twin was still there. Working in some sort of capacity with some sort of contracted agency.

She took Luna back to the SUV, settled her in the rear, and climbed in behind the wheel.

"Everything okay?" Everett asked.

"Yes, I feel better that Luna alerted again in the same two areas. Sitting on the employee entrance is our best chance at finding Zoe." She put the SUV in gear and left the parking lot.

"If you'd rather take the first shift, that's fine with me," Everett said.

"You can take it." She told herself that working the later shift provided a better opportunity to find her sister. Even though the idea of sitting for several hours at the cabin doing nothing would be pure torture. "While you're staking the place out, I'll do some searching on contract employee companies, maybe one of them advertised being hired by the Denali Grand Chalet."

"That's a good idea. If I had a list of companies that we knew for sure had employees working at the Chalet, I can ask Trent to try for another search warrant."

Helena grimaced. "That might be too late. If it takes two days to get another search warrant, we'll end up missing the grand opening tomorrow night."

Everett sighed. "I'll see if my buddy can put a rush on it."

"Maybe we should both search the companies, might be quicker in the long run." She glanced at him. "Staking out the hotel is a long shot, Everett. We could have already missed Zoe going in and it could be hours before she comes back out."

"I know." He pursed his lips. "Okay, we'll do the search first and then set up the hotel watch."

Helena scowled. This case was proving to be more difficult than most, and not just because Zoe was her sister.

It shouldn't be this difficult to find out who worked for what company. No wonder the string of thefts had gone unresolved for so long.

She turned her attention to the road, eyeing the vehicles behind her. Spotting a tail on Denali Park Road was impossible thanks to the large busses hogging the roads. It wasn't easy to see beyond them.

When their turnoff approached, she decided to drive past it, to come at it from the other direction. Just in case.

They needed their safe house to remain just that—safe and well hidden.

Christine began to fuss, making her feel guilty. It wasn't time to eat, but the baby may need to be changed, or was sick of being in her infant carrier.

"Don't worry, she's fine," Everett said when she kept glancing at the rearview mirror. "Better to make sure we're not followed."

"I know." She turned off at the next available road and drove for a mile before doubling back. Christine was building up to a full-blown crying fit by the time she pulled onto the long, winding driveway to their cabin.

Luna didn't like the baby's crying and began to whimper, too.

"Take it easy, we're home," Everett said, as if the baby, and Luna for that matter, could actually understand him.

"I'll take the baby, you grab the diaper bag and Luna," Everett said, jumping out and reaching for the door handle. "That girl has a healthy set of lungs."

"Yeah." And anyone within listening distance who knew they had Zoe's baby could likely hear her crying, too.

Spurred by a sense of urgency, Helena quickly freed Luna from the back of the SUV and grabbed the diaper bag and the dog's dishes before following Everett and Christine inside.

Luna hadn't growled a warning, which made her feel better.

Everett unbuckled the baby and held her, rubbing her back in a soothing manner. "Hey now, it's okay. See? Everything is just fine."

Christine's crying softened in volume as he continued to talk to her. Helena's heart did a funny little flip in her chest as she watched him interact with the baby, talking to her even as he pulled a diaper from the bag and prepared to change her.

Everett had the role of doting father down pat, and Christine wasn't even his child.

She sensed his actions were based on long-dormant instincts that had risen to the surface the minute he was confronted with a crying infant.

And it hurt to think about how he still blamed himself for the loss of his wife and son.

Especially since he clearly had so much love yet to give.

And wasn't love God's greatest blessing?

Everett was glad when Christine quieted down, seemingly content especially after he'd changed her, then set her on a blanket stretched out on the floor. He'd made a bottle, but she hadn't been interested in that, so he'd set it aside for later.

"Have you heard of a place called Right-Source?" Helena asked, staring down at her phone screen.

"No, are you sure it's not The Right One?" He moved away from the baby. "That's the agency I looked into previously. They were hired to help staff the anniversary party, where a large amount of jewelry and cash was stolen."

"I'm sure it's RightSource and, interestingly

enough, it looks as if they're helping to staff another hotel here in Denali." She met his gaze. "Not the Grand Chalet, but the Lodge."

"Interesting." He pulled up the information on his own phone. RightSource was so similar to The Right One, he couldn't help but wonder if the company had simply changed its name. It had been one of his theories all along that these companies kept morphing or changing hands, but the people working there were all the same.

"Do you think it's possible that the hotel managers share staff between them?" Helena asked. "There's another agency, by the name of RightChoice, that is being used by another Denali hotel. But again, not the new one. Still, it makes me think they might share staff."

"Maybe." He thought of how smug Ms. Farnsworth had been when he'd questioned her about contracted agencies. Was that because she didn't use them directly, but shared with others? "I wouldn't put anything past that woman I dealt with."

"She'll be singing a different tune if we prevent a big theft," Helena pointed out.

"I know." Still the HR director's attitude bothered him. He decided to call Trent.

His buddy answered with a groan. "Don't tell me you need another favor."

"I'm sorry, man, but the warrant was a bust.

We now think that Zoe Maddox is working for one of the contracted agencies. If I get you a list, do you think the judge will approve?"

"I don't know," Trent said honestly. "I mean, I used the K-9 finding the scent and the grand opening of the hotel as leverage. Not sure that will fly with your attempt to cast a broader net."

"Will you at least try?" Everett figured it was worth a shot. "We want to add RightSource, RightChoice and—" He glanced at Helena, who showed him her phone and the agency listed there. "Temporary Solutions."

"Three agencies?" Trent's voice rose incredulously.

"I know it's a stretch, but please, man. If we don't find Zoe soon, we'll lose our best chance to break this case wide open."

"Yeah, pretty sure you told me that last time, only to come up empty-handed," Trent groused. "Fine, I'll try. I'll head over there right after lunch. But don't hold your breath, Brand. This is not a sure thing by any means."

"I hear you loud and clear. Thanks, Trent, I owe you one."

"You owe me two," Trent corrected before disconnecting.

"He'll do his best," he said in response to

Helena's questioning gaze. "But he's not convinced the judge will go for it."

She nodded. "That's all we can ask for, I guess. I'll take Luna out one more time, then you can head over to do the first watch on the Chalet."

"Sounds good." He stood then froze when Luna began to growl.

Helena was already on her feet and sliding up to the window, weapon in hand.

Instinctively expecting the worst, he swept Christine up off the floor and tucked her into the infant carrier. Then he stuffed the bottle and supplies into the diaper bag.

Luna stared at the doorway, her nose quivering, low growls still emanating from her throat.

"See anything?" he whispered.

She stared for so long then eased back from the window, her face pale. "The front tires of the SUV are flat as pancakes." Her voice was barely loud enough to hear. "They've disabled the SUV."

"We're going out the back." Everett figured melting into the woods was their best chance of surviving. "Hurry."

Luna stayed close to Helena's side, and he was frankly much less worried about the dog alerting anyone to their presence.

The baby was an added complication.

They moved swiftly to the bedroom furthest from the front of the cabin. He eased open the window, which thankfully didn't make any noise. Everett slipped through the opening, then reached in and grabbed the infant seat. Helena followed and stepped back as Luna jumped out.

Without speaking, they made their way through the brush. Every one of Everett's senses were on high alert. If the tires were already flat, then he felt certain the shooter was nearby. Maybe had even gone around to the back of the cabin, where they were trying to disappear into the forest.

The only thing that helped hide their escape was the dark clouds swirling overhead. Afternoon storms weren't uncommon in July, the heat rose and wind over the ice-capped mountains often created a clash of atmospheric pressure.

As he moved from one tree to the next, he found himself praying. *Please God, guide us and protect us. Keep this sweet, innocent baby safe from harm.*

Helena stopped and held up a hand. He froze and then slowly dropped to a crouch so that he could set the infant carrier behind a thick bush. He was grateful that, so far, Christine hadn't begun to cry.

Helena gestured to the right, and he tracked

his gaze in that direction, trying to understand what had caught her attention.

There! A man wearing all black, was creeping up behind the cabin, getting close to the window they'd left open in their haste to get away.

With a frown, he realized the guy was not Gareth Cantwell, the man in denim who'd taken a shot at him.

This was a new player on the scene.

Suddenly a couple of things happened at once. The man saw the open window and turned to rake his gaze over the wooded area. Meanwhile, Christine began to cry, drawing the man's attention to their general hiding spot. When the shooter lifted his gun, Everett shouted, "Police! Drop your weapon!"

A sneer spread across the man's features and he didn't comply. Everett saw his finger tighten on the trigger, leaving him little choice but to return fire.

Twin gunshots echoed around them. Everett saw the man flinch, but that didn't stop him from running.

"Get him!" Helena shouted, and Luna took off like a shot, chasing the shooter. "Stay with Christine," she said to Everett before going after her partner.

He knelt beside the baby, his heart thundering in his chest, hoping and praying Helena and Luna would be safe while apprehending the guy.

He could be the link they needed to find Zoe.

ELEVEN

Helena pushed through the brush, following her partner and doing her best to keep her eye on Luna's bushy tail, which was all she could see.

Up ahead, the sound of a car engine gave her pause. Was the shooter getting away?

No! She quickened her pace, ignoring the branches that slapped at her face. But then she heard the sound of Luna's frenzied barking and the squeal of tires.

By the time she caught up with Luna, all she could see were the taillights of a retreating vehicle. Sharp disappointment stabbed deep.

"It's okay, girl." She bent to catch her breath, stroking a reassuring hand over Luna's thick pelt. Luna's gaze was still locked on the vehicle and Helena hoped the gunman hadn't kicked out at her partner, hurting her in some way.

She ran a hand over the K-9's face, reassured

that there were no injuries, when she noticed there was a bit of black fabric in Luna's mouth.

"Got close enough to get a piece of him, did you? Good girl, Luna. Good girl." She gently pried the material from her partner's mouth and placed it in a small evidence bag from her uniform pocket. Maybe it would come in handy down the road if there was another opportunity to track the shooter.

Resigned, she tried not to let the guy's escape wear her down. Luna was great at apprehending bad guys, and if there hadn't been a car waiting, her partner would have brought this one down, too.

They'd been *so close* to getting him. But all was not lost. There were droplets of blood on the ground here, indicating Everett's shot had hit its mark. She quickly used another evidence bag to pick up a blood-splattered leaf that could be used to obtain a possible DNA match.

Then, knowing there was no time to wallow in regret, she turned to head back to where Everett and Christine waited. "Come, Luna."

As she retraced her steps, the dog stayed close to her side. There were additional spots of blood, but she didn't bother to collect any further evidence. What they had was more than enough.

As she approached the area behind the cabin, she called out, "Everett? Where are you?"

"Here." He moved into view, his gaze raking over her. "You okay? Luna, too?"

"We are, but the shooter got away. There was a car waiting for him."

Everett looked dejected. "I was hoping we'd get key information from the guy."

"Me, too. But we have a few more clues, a sample of his blood and a bit of black denim from his jeans." She held up the twin evidence bags.

"That's good news but doesn't help us at the moment. We need to call for backup and get away from the cabin, ASAP." His expression turned grim. "The shooter could bring reinforcements, fanning out to find us."

"I know." It was a horrible thought. "We'll stay in the trees as we hike, see if we can find a spot to hunker down for a bit."

"I was thinking we could use someone from your K-9 Unit to provide backup," Everett said, lifting Christine's infant carrier. "I think they're better equipped for this kind of thing than the rangers."

She couldn't deny she preferred having her own team helping them. "I'll make the call, but the park rangers are much closer."

"I know." Everett glanced at her. "I just don't

understand how our safe houses keep getting compromised and in such short timeframes. Maybe I'm being paranoid, but I'm hesitant to trust anyone other than your K-9 team at the moment."

She nodded slowly. "Okay, that's fine with me. Do you want me to carry Christine for a while? Lugging that thing can't be easy."

"I have her." Everett's tone was firm. The muscles in his arms bunched and she hated to admit that she wouldn't be able to carry Christine through the thick brush for very long.

"We could try to fashion some way for Luna to help carry her," she offered as they headed deeper into the woods.

"Later." Everett glanced over his shoulder. "For now, I want to get far away from the cabin."

It was a good plan, so she concentrated on breaking a path for Everett. She hoped the shooter and his pals weren't experts on tracking through the forest, because she felt certain they were creating a path a blind man could follow.

But this area of the woods wasn't on the usual hiking trails, which meant the brush was thick and not easily slipped past.

She tried to take solace in the facts that they were both armed and that they had Luna with them. The way the shooter had run away from her K-9 made her think they didn't have a lot of experience with four-legged cops.

And Luna was better than most, in her humble opinion. Although she might be a bit biased about that.

The terrain became less rugged as it sloped upward. When she saw an opening between two jagged rocks, she lifted a hand to stop Everett. "Do you think that's a cave?"

"Could be." His muscles were bulging with the effort of lugging Christine's infant carrier, but his breathing was even, and she had to give him credit for being in such great physical shape. "I'll check it out."

Thinking he might need a break, she nodded. "Okay, that's fine. Luna and I will watch over Christine."

"She's been really good through all this," Everett said as he set the carrier on the ground. Luna immediately sat beside the baby, looking alert and on guard. "I was worried that she'd start crying again."

"I know." Going on the run with a baby was not something she'd anticipated, but here they were. As she watched Everett approach the opening, she remembered how Will Stryker and his K-9 partner, Scout, had found a cave her first day in Denali.

Gazing around, she tried to picture a map

of the area in her head. There had to be several caves in Denali, so it wasn't likely to be the same one. Not to mention the way they'd moved around to several different locations.

But, per her estimation, this cave wasn't that far from the hotels in the valley of Denali. If she was imagining the place correctly, the cluster of hotels would be located due west.

Christine began to squirm, so Helena bent and lifted the baby into her arms. "It's okay, sweetie. We're okay." She wished more than anything that they had access to a vehicle, but that wouldn't happen until backup arrived.

Even then, they'd have to hike out to meet up with the team. Or have the team hike in to meet them.

Everett was right to be concerned about how they kept getting found. It didn't make any sense. They'd been keeping a low profile and had never noticed anyone following them while driving to the hotel and back.

But there were always park ranger vehicles around. Was it possible Everett's paranoia was well founded in reality? She didn't want to believe that a park ranger would be involved in anything like this, but then again, it was odd that their hiding places were constantly being breached.

Everett returned a full fifteen minutes later.

"I didn't see any wildlife hiding in there, but there are a couple of tunnels I didn't take the time to fully explore. Having Luna with us should help, though. She'll sniff out anything I may have missed."

"Okay, I'll call for backup and we can take shelter in the cave while we wait." The storm clouds overhead were getting darker. "It's going to take a while for anyone from the K-9 Unit to get here, anyway."

"I know. Here, give me Christine while you make the call."

She pressed a kiss to the baby's temple before handing her over. It took a while for Katie Kapowski to answer the colonel's phone. "Katie? It's Helena. I need backup in Denali, ASAP. My police SUV is damaged, and I'm hiding in a cave with Officer Brand and Zoe's daughter."

"Oh, my, that doesn't sound good." She heard Katie typing in the background. "I think I can free up Will Stryker and Scout, but it may take a couple of hours. Please hold while I contact Lorenza. I know she'll want to talk to you."

"Okay." Glancing at the clouds, she covered the microphone with one hand. "Will you please take Christine into the cave? I'll be there shortly. I doubt there's cell service in there."

"Sure." Everett lowered the baby into the infant seat and strapped her in. Then he hoisted the carrier and made his way to the cave.

Luna whined in her throat, clearly torn between going along and staying near Helena.

"Helena? What's this about your vehicle being damaged?"

She quickly filled her boss in on the most recent events. "Everett shot the guy, but his wound must have been minor since he still managed to get away. I have his DNA, though, and a piece of his clothing."

"Okay, Katie has already called Will. He and Scout will be on the road within the next hour or so. I can try to pull another K-9 member off a current assignment if you think you need additional backup."

"Will and Scout are fine for now. The grand opening of the Denali Grand Chalet takes place in twenty-four hours. We may need more team members to cover that event and to help watch Christine."

"I'll make a note of it," Lorenza replied. "Although a couple of our other cases are heating up."

Helena thought about Everett's cop friend. "Everett has a fellow officer helping him, maybe we'll snag him for help, too. We'll make it work somehow."

"I know you will," Lorenza said reassuringly.

"Sit tight for a while. When Will gets close to Denali, he'll call you."

"Thanks." Helena disconnected the call. "Come, Luna." She hurried toward the cave opening, reaching it seconds before a light rain began to fall.

Great. They'd be stuck in the cave until it stopped. No way was she risking Christine's health by heading out into the rainfall.

She could only hope and pray they'd be safe from two-legged or four-legged threats, at least until backup arrived.

Everett scooped out the cave as best he could. There were signs that wildlife had been there in the past, but he hadn't run across any now.

He lifted a crying Christine from her carrier. The poor kid had been through a lot, being hauled through the woods, and she was likely hungry.

"I'll feed her," Helena offered as she walked Luna around the cave. So far, the K-9 wasn't acting skittish or giving any indication that they weren't alone in the small area.

Everett trusted Luna's scent better than his own attempt to check the place out.

Helena dropped to sit cross-legged on the ground near the carrier and gestured for the baby. He set Christine in her arms and then handed over the bottle he'd thankfully made prior to leaving the cabin.

"We're going to need to find fresh water for Luna," she said as Christine settled in. "She's worked hard and will become dangerously dehydrated with all that fur."

Fur that kept the K-9 warm in winter but evidently wasn't nearly as helpful in the brief summer months. He rummaged in the diaper bag and pulled out an empty wipes container. "I'll use this to capture rainwater."

"That should work," Helena said with a grateful smile.

He ended up getting wet as he waited for the container to fill partway with water. He then rinsed it out with the help of some leaves and waited for it to fill up again.

It took longer than he'd thought, considering the way the rain was coming down. Glancing at the clouds, he could see them swirling. How long would they be stuck here?

Hopefully not all night.

When the container was half full, he took it back in. "Do you think I could make a bottle for Christine first?"

"Good idea."

He prepared the bottle then took a drink of the water for himself, offering the rest to Helena. "We need to keep hydrated, too. I'll fill it up again for Luna."

When they'd quenched their thirst, he took the container outside and filled it again. Back inside the cave, he set it next to Helena, remembering what she'd said about the dog only taking food and water from her.

"Here, girl," she said encouragingly, offering the container to Luna.

The K-9 sniffed it then lapped up the liquid.

When she'd finished, Everett went back to the cave entrance for more. As he waited, he swept his gaze over the landscape. Thankfully there was no sign of anyone moving through the forest toward them. Maybe the rain would hold them off. He was thankful they had Luna to let them know if anyone came close.

Each time their safe house had been breached, Luna had provided the initial warning, alerting them with her low, rumbling growls. He appreciated how her keen ears and sense of smell was so much more useful than any of his senses.

He pulled out his phone and called his buddy Trent. "How do you feel about a trip to Denali?"

"What do you need?" Trent sounded happy to help as long as he wasn't about to be stuck doing more paperwork.

"We could use backup."

"Backup? What's going on?" the other man asked.

"We're stuck in the forest without a vehicle." He quickly filled Trent in on what had transpired. "Also, we'll need help covering the Denali Grand Chalet's grand opening event tomorrow night."

"I'm in," Trent said without hesitation. "Give me some time to follow up on that warrant, and I'll hit the road. And stay safe, man."

"Thanks, I really appreciate it." Everett ended the call and put his phone back in his pocket.

When the container was three-fourths full, he carried it back inside and dropped down beside Helena and Christine.

"Is the rain letting up?" Helena asked.

"Not yet." He hesitated before saying, "I've been wondering about these attacks. Doesn't it seem as if they've had more than one opportunity to kill us, if that was truly part of their plan?"

Helena's green eyes grew thoughtful. "You're right. There have been more near misses than actual harm."

"Exactly. They've fired at us several times, but have only hit the SUV, not either of us." He had to pull his gaze from the sweet image of

Helena feeding Christine, with Luna stretched out beside them. For the first time since they'd been together with the baby, he didn't look at Helena and think of Sheila.

Instead, he looked at Helena, wishing for the opportunity to steal another kiss.

That was pure craziness. He wasn't interested in heading down that path. So why couldn't he get the brief but heated kiss out of his mind?

"Do you think Christine is the real target?" Helena's question brought him back to the case.

"Maybe." He frowned and pulled the diaper bag over as a thought struck. "Or maybe they're somehow tracking us through the baby."

Helena sucked in a harsh breath. "I never thought of that."

He hadn't, either. What did that say about his skill as a cop? Not much. With systematic thoroughness, he removed items from the pink diaper bag, checking everything for a hidden tracker or chip of some sort.

Nothing in the full container of wipes, or the diapers, or the cans of formula. He pulled out the note and the birth certificate Zoe had left, examining each closely as if he may have missed some sort of clue. But came up empty. Even the seams of the diaper bag were clean. No evidence of tampering that he could see.

"Nothing," he muttered as he started putting everything back into the diaper bag.

"Maybe check the infant carrier, just to make sure," Helena suggested.

That had been his next thought, too.

Once he had the diaper bag returned to a semblance of order, he checked the plastic infant carrier. The cushions were made of plastic, easily cleanable and without any sign of being cut open and fastened shut. The pink-and-blue animal design was contiguous, as well. Turning the infant carrier over, he found the rest of it to be constructed of a thicker, heavier plastic. There was absolutely nothing to indicate someone had slipped something inside.

"It's clean," he said with a sigh. Knowing there was nothing there should have made him feel better.

Only it didn't.

At least, if they'd found a tracker of some sort, they could ditch it and feel safe moving forward.

But that clearly wasn't happening.

"I wish I knew how they keep finding us," he said on a weary sigh.

"Me, too." Helena had finished feeding the baby and had her sitting on her lap so that Christine could look around at her surroundings.

Her bright, curious eyes made him smile. At

least the baby was too young to be frightened
by everything going on.

"Maybe these thugs have better technical
skills than we're giving them credit for," Helena said. "I mean you spoke twice to your contact, could be that he's the link."

"Maybe." Anger vibrated through him. This
little girl shouldn't be in danger. All innocent
children should be protected from harm.

"You know, I wonder if they're trying to get
Christine to use as leverage to force Zoe into
continuing to work for them," Helena said in a
low voice filled with concern. "It would explain
why she left Christine with us. And, if they're
not out to kill us, then getting the baby back is
the only theory that makes sense."

"You could be right about that." It bothered
Everett to think that the baby was nothing more
than a pawn in all this. "On the other hand,
simply threatening the baby would have the
same effect, don't you think?"

Helena lifted a shoulder in a helpless gesture.
"Zoe might not believe them, having faith in
our ability to keep her daughter safe."

Faith was one thing he had in short supply.
He'd already failed once to keep his wife and
son safe.

He wouldn't survive if he failed, again.

TWELVE

Helena held the baby close. The more she thought about the events going on around them, she grew convinced that the baby was the ultimate target.

That was horrifying in and of itself. What kind of person targeted a three-month-old baby?

Gareth Cantwell? Or someone else higher on the food chain within the criminal organization?

A loud crack echoed from somewhere outside the cave. She froze and locked gazes with Everett.

"Take Christine to the back of the cave," he whispered. "I'll check it out."

She nodded and slowly stood. Gripping the infant carrier with one hand, she eased along the cave wall. "Luna, come," she whispered.

The K-9 stayed close as if sensing danger.

Keeping her gaze trained on the opening,

she wished there was a way to provide Everett back-up. She couldn't send Luna as the dog probably wouldn't listen to him.

But the K-9 could guard Christine.

After strapping the baby into the carrier, she looked at Luna. "Guard."

Luna sat straight and tall next to Christine.

"Good girl. Guard, Luna." Satisfied her partner would do just that, Helena pulled her weapon and crept toward the cave opening.

The rain had softened to a light drizzle. Peering through the woods, she tried to find Everett. But he wasn't anywhere nearby.

It was as if the forest had swallowed him.

She carefully made her way through the brush, listening intently. The crack had likely been the snapping of a tree branch, and she was afraid that meant the bad guys were still out there, searching for them.

For Christine.

A flash of something blue caught her eye. She instinctively swiveled toward it and dropped to the ground; her weapon aimed in that direction.

For long moments there was nothing. Then a man emerged from the brush.

Everett.

After a moment of sagging relief, she stood to catch his attention. He looked surprised to see her, but quickly made his way toward her.

"Find anything?" She whispered.

"A large tree branch lying on the ground about thirty yards from here." His voice was soft. "I can't say for sure if it fell on its own or had help from man or beast."

She raked her gaze over the woods. "It's likely they're searching for us."

"I know. But I didn't stumble across anyone, so it could be they're moving off in the wrong direction. Let's get back inside the cave."

She followed as he retraced their steps to return to the cave. She quickly went over to where Luna was still guarding Christine. "Good girl," she praised her partner, giving the animal a quick rub.

"We need to leave soon," Everett said, his expression grim. "The rain isn't too bad and it will take us longer to navigate through the woods carrying Christine."

"Agreed. I'm sorry you've been stuck with the heavy lifting. I don't mind taking turns."

"I'm fine. How long until your backup arrives?" Everett asked, changing the subject.

She glanced down at her phone, estimating the amount of time that had already passed. "At least four hours, maybe more. What do you think about getting one of your fellow officers to assist? Maybe Trent?"

Everett flashed a smile. "I'm way ahead of

you on that. I called him while I was waiting for the container to fill with rainwater. He had some things to tie up, as well, so it's likely he won't get here much before your teammate."

"That's reassuring to have additional back-up," Helena admitted. "The more cops helping us out, the better. Having Christine out in the middle of the woods makes us vulnerable."

"Yeah, I don't like it, either. But we'll keep her safe long enough for the others to arrive."

"Yes." She couldn't have asked for a better partner than Everett. Aside from Luna.

Everett came over and glanced down at the baby. "Make one more bottle for her before we go."

"Will do." She made Christine's bottle and then offered Luna more water. After she packed the diaper bag, she glanced around the interior of the cave. "You know, I wonder if this is the same cave Will Stryker and Scout found that first day."

"There are dozens of caves in Denali," Everett pointed out. "Many were old mining sites from the gold rush era. Those tunnels are wide enough and tall enough to allow people to move through them."

It was an intriguing thought. "How far back do they go?"

He shook his head. "I only went a few yards

in either direction, just looking for evidence of animals being here. It's interesting that there aren't many animal droppings, you'd think there would be."

That made her shiver. Growing up in Alaska, she'd had many close encounters with wildlife, mostly moose, elk and deer. She'd had also caught glimpses of bears and mountain lions from a distance.

But they had Christine's safety to worry about. This was not the time to run into a bear, mountain lion or a moose.

A female moose could be very aggressive, much like a bear, especially when protecting its young.

"I did notice the air was relatively fresh," Everett continued. "Which makes me think there's another cave opening on either end of the tunnels. If this was used back in the day by gold miners, they would absolutely want a second way out in case there was a tunnel collapse, which were fairly common."

She swallowed hard. No way would she want to be stuck in here.

"Ready?" Everett asked.

She nodded. There wasn't really another option. They couldn't just sit in the cave and expect their backup to find them. Especially not if the bad guys were out there, searching for them. They needed to meet Stryker and Trent halfway.

Everett lifted the carrier and gripped the blanket-covered handle. She slung the pink diaper bag over her shoulder and called to Luna.

"Come." Her K-9 partner came to stand beside her. "I think it's best if Luna and I take the lead," she told Everett. "Luna will alert us to danger, scenting the men searching for us before we see them and you'll be better equipped to protect the baby."

"Sounds good."

She appreciated how he didn't get into a macho argument with her over every little thing. Well, the exception being his insistence that he carry Christine. But she couldn't deny his arm strength was far superior to hers.

Why couldn't Kade have been like Everett? Why couldn't her ex have seen her as a partner instead of some weak woman who should wield a spatula rather than a gun?

She pushed through the wet branches, the water quickly soaking her uniform. Ignoring the discomfort, she followed what may have been a path someone else had taken not too long ago.

The rain had dropped the temperature to a nice seventy-two degrees, which would help keep them somewhat hydrated. They'd likely have to hike for a couple of hours, the little bit of rainwater they'd each consumed wouldn't hold them for long.

Her phone vibrated and she quickly grabbed it. "Maddox," she answered in a whisper.

"Helena? I'm about two hours outside Denali," Will said. "Traffic isn't bad, so I've been making good time."

"That's great news." She pushed another branch out of the way, holding it up for Everett and Christine. "We're hiking toward the hotels, and recently heard a noise in the brush making us think the bad guys are still out there, looking for us."

"I don't like hearing that," Will said.

"We plan to stay hidden in the brush until you show up."

"Good plan. I'll call you when I arrive."

"Thanks." She clicked off the call and glanced at Everett. "Will is only two hours away."

"Okay." He switched the infant carrier from one arm to the other. "Let's keep going."

They fell silent again as they continued through the damp forest. When Luna stopped to sniff what might have been a scant bit of dog feces left behind from someone's attempt to clean it up, she realized that this might have been the same area Will and Scout had been in.

The thought gave her hope that they were headed in the right direction. "Come, Luna."

Her K-9 turned from the scent and fell into step beside her.

The terrain was rocky and full of hazards. When she came across some of the larger branches covering the meager path, she called out a warning to Everett.

Up ahead, she couldn't see any sign of the hotels, their ultimate destination. Had she underestimated the distance? Maybe.

She continued pushing forward, determined to get them out of there. She'd feel better once they met up with Stryker, but where on earth would they find yet another place to stay? Considering they'd been through three cabins so far, she wasn't hopeful they'd easily find another.

What if they actually rented rooms in the hotel? Maybe not under her name or Everett's, but Will or Trent could secure a room. If there were any available.

That may be the sticking point, especially with the grand opening tomorrow evening.

She shook off the depressing thought and slapped at a mosquito. The colonel might be able to find a way to make it happen.

But first, they needed to get out of the woods, before the bad guys caught up to them.

And without getting lost. Not now. Not when they were so close.

Dear Lord, guide us to safety.

Everett's biceps and shoulders were screaming in pain from lugging the infant carrier, but he did his best to ignore the discomfort.

They'd be out of the woods soon, right?

Right.

These infant seats weren't meant for hiking through rough terrain, that's for sure. But he wasn't going to leave it behind, either. The poor kid had to sleep somewhere.

He had no idea where they'd be spending the rest of the night, except maybe in Will Stryker's or Trent's SUV.

The sky overhead was still light, but according to his watch—and his stomach—it was close to dinner time.

Helena stopped and raised a hand in warning. He froze, casting his gaze around for what might have caught her attention.

Then he heard Luna's low growls. A sinking feeling settled in his gut. No way could they outrun the bad guys while carrying Christine.

Moving as quietly as possible, he set Christine down and stood in front of her, weapon at the ready, determined to protect the baby with his life if necessary.

Helena had her weapon out, too, but then he noticed she knelt on the ground beside Luna, her arm slung over the dog's shoulders.

What had caught the K-9's attention?

"Go!" Helena commanded.

Luna took off through the brush, barking at whatever was up ahead.

Everett stayed in front of Christine, even if he didn't quite understand what was going on.

Then he caught a glimpse of a large ram with impressive horns running through the trees. Some of the tension eased, but he kept the animal in sight, hoping it didn't turn and charge at Luna.

Instead, it turned and made a loop around some trees, heading toward him and Christine.

He leveled his weapon, not wanting to hurt the beautiful ram. At the last minute, the large animal turned and disappeared from view.

Helena called the dog back. "Come, Luna. Heel!"

Looking dejected, the K-9 turned and ran back to them. Helena praised the dog, gave her a treat and then rose.

He lifted Christine and came toward her. "Luna was awesome."

"Yeah, although when she first started growling, I was afraid one of the shooters had found us." Helena puffed out a breath. "I was glad to see it was only the ram."

"It was a big one, so it's good you had Luna chase it off. Rams are known to charge humans if they feel their turf has been threatened."

"I know." She looked around the area. "I wish I could see at least one of the hotels."

"I have a pretty good sense of direction, and I believe we're on the right track," he assured her.

"Okay, I trust you." She turned back. "Come, Luna, let's keep going."

The brief respite from carrying Christine didn't provide much relief. But after another thirty minutes of hiking, he caught a glimpse of a hotel.

"Helena? Do you see it?" he called softly.

"Yes." She picked up the pace.

He swallowed a groan, shifted Christine to his other hand and told himself to be glad there hadn't been any sign of the bad guys since leaving the cave.

Yet.

Helena abruptly stopped again, this time edging behind the trunk of a large tree. She glanced back and gestured for him to join her.

"That's the road up ahead," she murmured. "We need to stay here, using the tree for cover until Will and Scout call."

He set Christine down and knelt beside her

carrier, lifting the blanket to check on how she was doing. She was sleeping, which was a blessing.

"Okay." He shooed away a mosquito and covered her up. "He should be here soon."

She nodded and pulled out her phone. "I'm running low on battery, so I hope he gets here before it shuts down."

Technology was wonderful, until it wasn't. A quick glance at his phone proved he was in the same predicament.

They stayed behind the tree for fifteen minutes before Helena's phone vibrated. "Will?" she asked in a whisper.

"Coming up Denali Park Road now," her colleague said in a voice loud enough that Everett could hear. "ETA five minutes."

"Thanks. We'll head out of the woods as soon as I see your SUV," Helena responded. "Official or personal?"

"Personal, it's black."

"Got it." She slid her phone into her pocket and glanced at him. "You heard?"

"Yes, black SUV." He looked at Luna. "Will your K-9 be okay in the same car?"

"Hopefully, since it won't be for long." She rested her hand on Luna's scruff. "At some point I'll need to have my old vehicle towed in for repair."

A black SUV rolled into view on Denali Park Road. Taking note of the K-9 in the back, Everett stood. "He's here."

"Good news," Helena muttered.

They made good time closing the gap. Still, at the edge of the woods, Helena hesitated, casting her gaze around the area.

"Go, I'll provide cover," Everett told her.

"Okay." She took the infant carrier from his grasp and quickly headed up to Will's black SUV. She placed Christine in first then gave Luna the signal to jump in.

When she was in the back seat beside Luna and Christine, he ran forward, taking the front passenger seat. The interior of the SUV was cool and a wave of relief washed over him when Will hit the gas.

They'd made it!

"Thanks for coming, Will." Helena removed the blanket covering Christine's carrier. "That was a close one."

"I can see that." Will glanced at Everett. "Good to see you again, Brand."

"Same here. Especially after being in the cave and the forest."

"Cave?" Will's eyebrows rose. "Was there a large room, with two tunnels branching off on either side?"

"Yeah." He eyed the K-9 cop. "We wondered if it might be the same one you found, although I'm sure there are dozens of them."

"Yes, but it's interesting because I came out of the woods in a completely different spot than you just did." Will glanced at Helena through the rearview mirror. "Oh, by the way, the colonel has arranged for us to stay in a large suit at the Denali Grand Chalet."

Everett's jaw dropped. "How on earth did she manage that?"

The other man shrugged. "She knows a lot of people around the state, I'm sure she leveraged the grand opening as a potential criminal magnet and demanded to have a police presence on the property." Will hesitated then added, "Although she did mention she's running out of favors, so this better be the last one."

"It's not our fault the safe houses have been compromised," Helena protested.

"I know, but the colonel made it clear she's running out of options," Will said. "I brought my personal SUV because it sounds like we may be working undercover on this assignment. If we don't find Helena's sister before the grand opening, Lorenza wants us to attend as guests."

"Guests?" Helena echoed with a frown. "I'll need something to wear."

That made Everett chuckle. "We all will, Helena. Right now, we couldn't even pass as cops in these drenched and stained uniforms."

"True," Will agreed.

Everett's phone rang and he quickly answered. "Hey, Trent, what's your ETA?"

"Thirty minutes," his buddy responded. "Where should I meet you?"

"The Denali Grand Chalet." He explained about the suite the leader of the K-9 Unit had arranged for them. "Call me when you get here, and I'll give you the room number."

"Okay, that's a plan." There was a pause then Trent said, "Bad news on the warrant."

He momentarily closed his eyes. "The judge shot it down."

"Yep, said it was too broad. If we could narrow it down to one contract company, he'd reconsider."

"Okay, thanks for trying." Everett slipped his phone into his pocket, unable to hide his disappointment.

"No warrant?" Helena prompted.

"Nope." He turned in his seat to glance at her. "We'll have to find Zoe another way."

She nodded, although he could see the despair in her eyes.

After running from three safe houses, they were right back where they'd started.

With no leads, other than the Denali Grand Chalet itself, on finding Zoe.

THIRTEEN

Helena knew the warrant had been a long shot, but she was still disappointed.

The only good news? She could use Luna to pick up Zoe's trail within the hotel. Maybe that would give them a clue as to where her twin was working, as a maid or as a server in the restaurant.

Yet if the grand opening was the ultimate target, time was running out. They needed a break in the case, and soon.

Will parked his black SUV near the main lobby. "I need you to stay here while I secure the room keys."

"What about the dogs?" Everett asked. "They're not going to let them inside."

Will flashed a grin. "We have a suite on the main level, so that we can easily take the dogs outside as needed. They're well behaved enough that we should be okay."

"We can always use the fact that we're state

troopers if necessary," Helena added. "You'd think the owner would be grateful to have a police presence."

"Not so sure about that." Everett shrugged. "I'll defer to your expertise."

Scout whined when Will left the SUV. Luna and Scout had been sniffing each other non-stop during the short drive, even though they worked together on a regular basis.

"He'll be back soon," Helena assured the K-9, leaning over to check on Christine. "Hi, sweetie, looks like you're awake."

"She okay?" Everett asked.

"Yes. Thankfully, it doesn't seem as if she's been too traumatized by recent events."

Everett reached up to massage his shoulder, his expression wry. "Probably felt like she was on a giant swing."

"Thank you, Everett." Oddly enough, now that they were safe, tears stung Helena's eyes. "I wouldn't have been able to do any of this without you."

His sweet, dark brown gaze clung to hers for a long moment and she remembered the warmth of his kiss. "I'm glad to be here, Helena. I have to admit, we make a pretty good team."

"We do." A partnership that would end as soon as they busted up the criminal ring and likely arrested Zoe. Her gaze landed back on Christine, who was shaking her plastic key rattle before bringing them to her mouth.

This precious little girl didn't deserve to be in the center of danger like this.

She looked back up at Everett. "Do you think I should hand the baby over to child protective services?"

He frowned. "Is that what you want?"

"No. Of course not. But we've been running from gunmen for several days now, and it's probably not fair for me keep Christine with me."

"I understand where you're coming from, Helena, but if Cantwell or his boss wants Christine, don't you think we're better prepared to keep her safe?"

Everett had a point. "I guess we've managed to do that so far."

"Look, this is almost over. The grand opening celebration has to be the next target." His gaze turned thoughtful. "Maybe catching them in the act is a better plan. Although I really wish I knew where they'd hidden the stolen goods."

Helena thought about the cave they'd found, then instantly dismissed that idea. For one thing, the caves were four-plus hours from Anchorage, which is where most of the crimes had been committed. Would they have really driven the loot out there to hide it? Didn't seem likely.

And even if they had, why would Gareth Cantwell or his boss risk leaving the stuff in a cave that could easily be inhabited by wild animals? Easy to imagine a wolf or a bear hanging out near the cave entrance, thwarting the bad guy's ability to grab their stolen goods.

Will returned, holding up a set of four keycards. "We're all set, although the clerk made a big deal of some movie star backing out at the last minute, which is how we were able to get the place."

"I'm glad for our sake," Everett said wryly.

The other man slid behind the wheel and drove to the north side of the building, which was directly opposite from where the employee entrance was located. There was additional parking available and he pulled into an empty space and shut down the SUV.

"We're in a large two-bedroom suite," Will said, handing over the keycards. "Our room number is 1004."

"Got it." Helena unbuckled Christine's car seat then pushed open her door so Luna could jump down. Her wrinkled uniform was beyond repair. "We'll need to check out the gift shop and adjacent boutique, see if we can find something casual and dressy to wear."

Will nodded. "The colonel said we could charge everything to the room."

Helena carried Christine's infant seat, trailed by Luna as she followed Everett to their suite. Her teammate and Scout came to join them.

The suite was spacious enough, and each bedroom had its own bathroom. Both Luna and Scout sniffed around the entire suite, as if to make sure there was no hint of danger.

"You want to head to the boutique first?" Everett asked. "I'll watch Christine."

"Sure." She couldn't wait to get out of her damp uniform.

"Why don't you both go?" Will suggested. "I'll watch the kid."

Helena eyed him curiously. "What do you know about babies?"

"Not much, but I'm pretty sure I can manage while you pick up new clothes." He bent over the infant carrier and made a funny face. Christine smiled and reached up as if to grab his nose. "I'm also planning to order pizza from room service, if you're hungry."

"We're famished." Everett took her arm. "Come on, Helena. She'll be fine. It's not like we'll be gone for long."

The gift shop items were extremely pricey, far more than she would have paid in Anchorage. But this was the kind of place that catered to the rich, so she swallowed her protest and bought a casual change of clothes along with a few personal items like a hairbrush, toothbrush and other sundries.

Everett did the same, and they added everything to the room tab. The amount was staggering.

"Wow, that's outrageous," Helena whispered as they walked down the hall to their suite. "Who are these people staying here, anyway?"

"I don't know," Everett admitted. "But it's easy to see why this hotel has become a target."

Back in the room, she had enough time to shower and change before the pizza arrived. Will loaned them his phone cord so they could each charge their phone batteries. As they ate, they discussed their next steps.

"I can take Luna through the hotel, see if she alerts on Zoe's scent," Helena offered.

"That's a place to start," Everett agreed. "But we also need to think about how to cover the grand opening."

Will eyed them both. "You could dress up and blend in as a wealthy couple. That way you'd both be on the inside, while Scout and I can cover the outer perimeter."

"That's a good idea, they had fancy clothes in the boutique." Everett's cell phone rang. "Trent?

We're in room 1004. A fellow officer," he said in response to Will's questioning look.

Helena inwardly groaned. "I despise wearing heels. Why couldn't we infiltrate the place as servers? That would give us better access to the rest of the staff."

"Another good idea," Everett said before taking another slice of pizza.

She heartily preferred the role of being one of the staff members. It was also something that would likely get her closer to Zoe. "And what about Luna? And Christine?"

"Trent can watch Christine," Everett announced with a grin. "He won't like being assigned babysitting duty, but he'll help out as needed."

"That just leaves Luna." At the sound of her name, Helena's K-9 partner came over to sit beside her. She stroked the elkhound's springy fur. "I could try to keep Luna somewhere close by, maybe as a support animal? Although that would probably bring unwanted attention."

"We'll check the layout, see if that's a possibility," Will said. "If not, we can leave her in the suite with Trent and the baby."

She took another bite of her pizza, resigned to buying more clothing at the overpriced boutique.

In her mind, attending the party in any role

was a last resort. If she could somehow find Zoe prior to the big event, they'd know exactly who they were searching for.

Information that would enable them to bust the criminal ring wide open.

Everett knew Helena wasn't keen on the idea of attending the party as a couple and tried not to take her reluctance personally.

It was his problem that he'd been unable to forget their brief but powerful kiss. Why he'd suddenly become hyperaware of Helena after three years of keeping his focus on being a cop, was beyond reason.

He didn't like it.

But couldn't get her out of his mind, either.

Trent arrived and he quickly performed introductions. "Glad to have another set of hands," Will said with a grin.

"Happy to help," Trent assured them.

"Even if that means babysitting?" Helena teased.

Trent glanced at the baby. "I have a nephew about that age, so it's not like I don't know how, but I'd rather assist in bringing these guys down."

Everett nodded. "I get that, but you need to know that our current theory is that the baby has somehow become a target. So you can understand that protecting Christine is a big deal for us."

Trent scowled. "What kind of idiot targets a baby?"

"A bad one," Everett responded.

After they'd devoured the pizza and Helena had fed and changed Christine, they decided to get some rest. Tomorrow would be a big day, and they needed to be sharp if they were going to catch Cantwell, his boss and Zoe in the act.

For Helena's sake, he hoped she'd find Zoe before the big party. He wanted to give her twin a chance to come clean, to make a deal to avoid jail time.

Christine needed her mother.

Why did he care so much? The undeniable answer was that it wasn't just Helena who'd gotten stuck in his mind, the baby had wiggled her way into his rock of a heart. Seeing the baby laugh, gaze around in wonder, or even sleep, made it impossible for him to remain distant.

Having a family of his own wasn't part of his plan, but he wanted Zoe to have a chance to spend the rest of her life with her daughter.

And with Helena.

Exhaustion pulled him into slumber, a deep sleep that he hadn't experienced since arriving in Denali. Maybe it was the presence of two more cops backing them up, but when he awoke at seven in the morning, he bolted upright in surprise.

Trent was sleeping in the twin bed on the other side of the room, but he heard voices from the main area of the suite and hurried out to join Helena and Will.

She had taken Christine into her room and was already giving her a bottle. Meanwhile, her teammate was scanning the room service menu, his K-9, Scout, next to him.

"What do you feel like for breakfast?" Will asked. The guy seemed obsessed with food. "Looks like they offer a wide variety."

"Whatever is easiest," Everett said with a shrug. He sat beside Helena. "How did she sleep?"

"Great." She propped Christine up and rubbed her back. "Would you mind taking over for a bit? Will brought in dog food for Luna and Scout, but she needs to go out first."

"Sure." He readily took the baby. "Were you serious about having Luna track Zoe's scent?"

"Yes, we'll talk that through in a bit." Helena grabbed Luna's leash. "Come, Luna."

Everett grinned when Christine let out a loud burp. "Atta girl," he praised.

Will laughed. "That was a loud one." Then his expression turned serious. "I've been thinking about the party tonight. From what I can find online, they're expecting over a hundred guests. That's not going to be easy to cover with just the three of us."

"Do you think there are other team members that could get here in time to help out?" Everett gave Christine the rest of the bottle. "I wouldn't mind additional help, but it sounded like your K-9 team was stretched pretty thin."

The other man grimaced. "They are, but I'll check in with the colonel again. This could be our last big chance to get these guys."

"And to find Helena's twin sister," Everett added.

Trent joined them and, when Helena and Luna came back inside, they ordered breakfast.

"I'm going to walk the perimeter of the hotel with Scout this morning," Will said. "Helena, I understand you and Everett are going to take Luna around, as well."

"That leaves me with babysitting duty." Trent looked at Christine. "Although I'd like to walk the building myself at some point, just in case we need to make a quick getaway."

Everett nodded. "That's fine, we'll come back and relieve you in a couple of hours."

"I can relieve him, too," Will added. Then he frowned. "Not that I know much about caring for a baby."

"It's not hard," Trent said dryly. He finished

his breakfast and set the plate aside. "I don't care who relieves me, I just want to be able to check the place out before the big event."

Everett understood where his buddy was coming from. "Call me if you need anything." He glanced at Helena. "Ready?"

She nodded and then disappeared into the bedroom to fetch the evidence bag containing Zoe's scarf. Then he noticed she had a second, smaller bag, with a bit of black fabric in it.

They headed out into the hallway and Helena offered the bag to Luna, then gave the command.

Her K-9 partner trotted down the hall, pausing on occasion to sniff at various hotel room doors, but never for long. The animal moved quickly and soon they were near the lobby.

"Heel," Helena commanded, bringing Luna to her side. She lowered her voice. "We need to be in the area of the hotel the staff would be in."

"Let's go back toward the conference rooms," he suggested. "That's probably where they're holding the party, maybe Luna will find something there."

They took a different route to that section of the hotel, to give Luna an additional opportunity to pick up Zoe's scent, but again the animal didn't alert.

When they reached the grand ballroom, the

area had been cordoned off. He could see several workers setting up dozens of round tables, along with three different serving stations.

"What do you think?" he asked in a low voice. "Could Zoe be in there, working?"

"Maybe." Before he could stop her, Helena unclipped the rope baring their way, and took Luna through. He followed, prepared to be kicked out in short order.

But no one stopped them right away, although they did garner several curious glances.

Still, Luna didn't alert. They'd made it about halfway through the room, when a tall man sporting a dark glower crossed over to them.

"You can't be in here," he snapped. "I need you to leave right now."

"We were just curious as to the layout here," Everett said in a meager attempt to give Luna more time to pick up Zoe's scent. "Quite impressive."

"Guests are not allowed," the man repeated. His scowl deepened. "Especially not dogs."

"This is a working dog," Helena said. "Notice the K-9 logo on her vest? We're part of the security team keeping an eye on things tonight."

The man stiffened. "No one told me about any additional security."

Everett shrugged. "Talk to your boss, we just do what we're told."

The man glared at him for a long moment. "Maybe you are part of the security team, but you still need to leave until I've spoken with my boss."

"Okay, fine." Helena called Luna over. "But anything that gets stolen tonight is on you."

Everett hid a smile as they made their way out of the grand ballroom. "I think you hit on the perfect cover for tonight," he said in a low voice.

"What's that?"

"Security." It was so simple, he couldn't believe they hadn't thought of it before. "I'll see what we can do to get added to the security team."

"Sounds good. But for now, I need to find a spot close to the kitchen," she murmured. "I really think Zoe is working as a server."

"I've never been inside the kitchen of a hotel, but let's see what we can find." Everett glanced over and spied a side door. He tried to imagine where the employee entrance was located in relation to where they were standing. "Maybe the kitchen is behind the ballroom. Let's check the door over there."

Helena offered the scent bag to Luna one more time then commanded her to seek Zoe.

Luna put her nose down and began her zig zag pattern.

"It won't be easy to track indoors," she told him. "The scent cones are too narrow and there are so many of them."

Suddenly, Luna lunged forward, sniffing eagerly around the base of the doorway. Then she sat, looking up at her handler.

"Good girl!" Helena praised. "You're a very good girl."

Everett reached past Luna to try the door but, of course, it was locked. Then he pressed his ear to the doorframe. The muted sound of clanking dishes confirmed his suspicion.

"The kitchen is back here."

She nodded. "Zoe must be part of the kitchen serving crew."

"If so, she won't be there now, but later tonight," he felt compelled to point out.

"I know." Helena sighed. "Guess that means we'll have to catch her during the party."

It wasn't optimal, but at least they had a plan.

Everett could only hope everything would go off without a hitch.

FOURTEEN

Helena couldn't believe they'd gotten so close to finding Zoe, only to be put off by a locked door.

If they really *were* part of the security team, they'd be allowed everywhere in the hotel. Okay, so having a dog in the kitchen wasn't exactly sanitary, and likely violated all kinds of state health codes, but still.

"I need to call Colonel Gallo," Helena said while following Everett back to their suite. "She needs to get us on the security team as soon as possible. That's our best chance of catching Zoe before the party."

"Okay, but you do realize your sister may not be working until later, right?" Everett glanced at her as he unlocked the door with the keycard. "I mean, it's not likely she'd be working early in the morning and throughout the day until whatever hour this party ends."

She gave a slight shrug of her shoulders. "I

know. But maybe we can intercept her when she arrives for work. Surely she'll get here before the party starts."

"Okay, make your call." He opened the door and waited for her and Luna to precede him inside. "It may take a few hours to get this all figured out anyway."

"Find anything?" Trent asked.

"Just more evidence that Zoe is working here." Everett looked over at Christine. "She give you any trouble?"

"Not at all." His buddy stood and stretched. "I'm going to do my own walk around the hotel."

"Go ahead." Helena waved her hand. "Better go now, because it's likely we'll need to head out again in the next hour or so."

Trent nodded and left the suite. She called Lorenza, watching as Everett took Christine out of her carrier and set her on a blanket that was stretched out on the carpeted floor.

"Hi, Helena. What's going on?" her boss asked.

"Luna alerted on a doorway leading into the kitchen, so we feel certain Zoe is working here as a server. The door was locked, though, so we didn't get inside. I think it might be helpful to have both Everett and I brought on board as security personnel. Any idea how to make that happen?"

"Security would give you access to the entire hotel," Lorenza agreed. "Let me make a few calls, see what I can do."

"Thanks." Helena let out the breath she hadn't been aware she'd been holding. "I think we're very close to breaking this case wide open."

"Understood. The only problem I foresee is that the hotel owner prefers to run things his own way." Lorenza's tone was wry. "He thinks money buys him the best security, but he's wrong about that."

She didn't even want to think about what would happen if the billionaire refused to let them be a part of his security team. "Hopefully common sense will prevail in the long run. Keep me posted."

"Will do." The colonel disconnected from the line.

"Problems?" Everett asked.

"Maybe." She updated him on what her boss had said. "Do we need a plan B in case she can't get this to work?"

"We could act as servers, as you'd originally suggested, but that would limit our ability to use Luna," Everett pointed out. "And her skills have been invaluable to this case."

"Yes, they have." She ran her fingers through the elkhound's fur. Thankfully, Will had a good supply of dog food, so both K-9s had been well fed and were ready to work. "Luna is our best chance of finding Zoe."

There was a slight pause before Everett said, "When we find your sister, you'll need to convince her to cooperate with us to circumvent jail time."

She glanced up in surprise. "Really? You think there's a possibility she can avoid being arrested?"

He grimaced. "She might be arrested, Helena, but if she cooperates, I'll work with the DA to minimize her sentence."

His offer warmed her heart. "I'm glad you're willing to do that, Everett. Thank you."

He offered her a crooked smile. "It's better for Christine to have her mother."

"Yes." She swallowed the lump in her throat. "And it seems pretty clear they're using her daughter to make her cooperate."

Minutes crept past slowly, to the point Helena was practically crawling out of her skin by the time Colonel Gallo returned her call.

"I hope you have good news," Helena said by way of greeting.

"I do. The guy in charge of security is Ben Watterson. He wasn't happy, but finally agreed to let you and Everett fill in as part of the security team."

She closed her eyes in relief. "Thank you so much."

"Yeah, well don't thank me yet. He wants to meet with the two of you and didn't sound at all happy about having a dog involved."

Helena glanced at Luna stretched out next to Christine. It was uncanny the way the K-9 seemed to understand it was her duty to protect the baby. "We'll convince him that it's only to his advantage."

"True, but I was thinking that maybe you'll be less noticeable without your K-9," Lorenza said slowly. "We don't want to tip them off as to your being there."

Her boss had a point, but she couldn't imagine working without her partner as backup. "We'll find a way to use Luna while keeping a low profile."

There was a slight hesitation before the older woman said, "Okay, I'll trust your judgment on this."

"When do we meet with Watterson?" Helena asked.

"He's expecting you both at noon."

"Perfect." Helena looked at Everett. "Thanks again for all your help on this case."

"Just get it done," Lorenza said gruffly. "And

call me with any updates." Her boss treated them like family but wasn't one for mushy stuff.

"Okay, thanks again." After ending the call, she filled Everett in on their plan to meet with Ben Watterson at 12:00 p.m.

"The security office is a few doors from the human resources' office space," Everett said with a grin. "I hope I get a chance to say hello to Ms. Farnsworth. She'll be oh so happy to see me."

"Not," Helena added with a smile. Then she frowned. "I wonder if we'll need to buy our own uniforms or if they'll provide them."

"We'll figure it out." Everett gestured to Luna. "I heard what you said about using Luna in security while keeping a low profile. Are you sure it's a good idea to have the K-9 involved?"

"I'm not sure about anything," she confessed. "We can blend in with the security team better without Luna, but I can't see leaving her behind."

"Except that the dog would provide another layer of protection for the baby," Everett noted. "Something to think about."

"Yeah, for sure." She was troubled by the conundrum. What if seeing Luna scared the bad guys off? Would they pick a new target, forcing them to start all over again? To have come this far without bringing the person in charge of these crimes to justice was unfathomable.

"Maybe there's a place I can keep her nearby," Helena said. "So that I can get to her quickly if needed."

"Maybe." Everett didn't sound hopeful.

Frankly, she wasn't feeling good about the possibility, either. For one thing, they'd have to be able to freely move around the hotel to figure out who and what might be the main target.

Helena closed her eyes and lifted her heart in prayer.

Guide me on Your path, Lord. Show me the way.

Everett moved over to where Helena stood with her chin down and her eyes closed. He rested his hand on her shoulder, offering comfort.

"We'll figure it out, Helena," he said in a low voice.

"I know." She lifted her head and smiled at him. "I've decided to put this dilemma in God's hands."

In recent years, he'd have scoffed at such an idea, but since being paired up with Helena the past few days, he was beginning to realize that maybe God was still watching over him, despite the way he'd turned his back on Him.

Everett had been the one to stop attending church services. And praying.

Until recently. Christine being in danger had sent him back into his former ways of coping.

And that included instinctively praying in times of trouble.

"I know it's difficult for you to believe," Helena said softly, "but I know God is watching over us, keeping us safe."

He gently squeezed her shoulder. "I still find it difficult to understand why God took my wife and son from me, but I can't argue that we've been blessed so far on this journey, escaping danger at every turn and finding new places to stay. Maybe it's a good idea to put this in God's hands."

A broad smile bloomed on her face. "I'm so glad to hear you say that."

Helena was so beautiful, her green eyes mesmerizing. Stepping closer to him, she lifted her face and, before he could pull away, she closed the gap and kissed him.

He gathered her to him, deepening the kiss. He could have cradled her in his arms like this forever, but the click of the door unlocking had them jumping apart like guilty teenagers.

Trent entered the room, eyeing them with a raised brow. "Something up?"

"Huh? Oh, no." Everett hoped his buddy

couldn't see the wild beating of his heart. Why couldn't Trent have waited just a few more minutes before bursting in? "Glad you're back, though. We have a meeting with the head of security at noon."

"Security? Good call." Trent pocketed his keycard. "The place is really big and spread out—it won't be easy to cover for a possible theft."

"I know." He cleared his throat, unable to meet Helena's gaze for fear his feelings would be broadcast for everyone in the entire hotel to see. "We're going to focus on trying to find Helena's twin sister, which should help."

The other man nodded slowly but, before he could say anything more, Will and Scout entered the suite. Luna jumped up and went over to greet her fellow K-9 in a way that made him smile.

"How did it go?" Helena asked.

"I have a good map of the exterior in my head," Will said as he filled Scout's bowl with water. "And you know, I found the entrance to the cave Scout and I found the first time we were here."

Everett glanced at Helena. "Like the one we were in?"

"Similar probably, but remember I mentioned I came out of the woods in a different spot. This cave is located several yards from the back of the hotel," Will explained.

He frowned. "That's the complete opposite direction."

"There are many caves here, thanks to the old mining days." Will shrugged. "And who knows? They could be connected. Honestly, I didn't go very far inside."

"I can't blame you for not wanting to go in too deep. Those tunnels have been around for a long time, no telling how stable they are." Everett glanced at his watch. "Helena, it's almost time for our meeting with Watterson."

"I know." She took a moment to fill her teammate in on their role as being members of the security team and clipped a leash to Luna's collar. Then she straightened and met Everett's gaze, a faint blush tinging her cheeks. "Let's go."

He held the door open for her then shut it behind them. He wanted to say something about their kiss but couldn't seem to think of a way to broach the subject as they walked.

"I keep thinking about those tunnels." Helena's voice broke into his thoughts.

"What about them?"

She shrugged. "It seems like Cantwell, or his boss, may be using them to get around Denali. It's a good way to stay off Denali Park Road and remain hidden from view. And it explains how the guy who'd left the hotel employee entrance had disappeared. He may have gone into the cave."

She seemed determined to keep the conversation on a professional level. "You have a point, and it could be how they followed us without our noticing."

"Exactly." Helena glanced at Luna. "I wish we'd found them earlier. Now it's almost too late to explore them."

"Just remember, Luna didn't alert on Zoe's scent in the cave we were in a few hours ago," he said, leading the way to the security office. "For now, the party is still our best option."

"You're right." She squared her shoulders. "Let's meet our new temporary boss."

Ben Watterson was former military and no-nonsense all the way. He stared at Luna for several long moments before meeting their gazes.

"I have uniforms for you to use and radios, but I have reservations about the dog."

"Luna is well trained," Helena assured him. "She's no different than some of the K-9s used in the military."

"Okay, fine." He waved a hand. "But if I hear complaints, she's gone."

"Understood," she agreed.

Everett still wasn't convinced that having

Luna with them would help them stay undercover, but there was time yet for Helena to figure out what to do. "What time does this shindig start?"

"Seven o'clock this evening, but I'll want you here dressed and ready to go by six."

"That's not a problem," he assured the other man.

They both got fitted for their uniforms, which turned out to be black slacks and shirts, with a security logo on the breast pocket. It felt odd to wear a uniform that wasn't issued by the Anchorage PD, and he could tell Helena was just as uncomfortable.

When they were finished with their uniforms, they were led to a table where there were several earbud devices connected to a radio so they could keep in contact with other members of the security team. After each of them taking one, there was one radio left, and Everett subtly pocketed it without anyone noticing.

Afterward they hauled everything back to the suite, to join Trent and Will. "They gave us radios," Everett explained. "I have an extra one for you, Will, for when you're stationed outside the premises. They use channel five, and you can listen in on that one, too, to know what'd going on. But if we want to talk without them listening in, use channel eight."

"Good idea," Will agreed. "Five for the hotel team and eight for us, alone. I like having the ability to chat amongst ourselves if needed."

"Me, too." Everett watched as Helena fed Christine. All they could do now was wait until it was time to report for duty.

And pray that they'd find Zoe.

Stomach knotted with tension, Helena changed into her security uniform. She figured she'd leave Luna in the suite for now, until she understood exactly what her assignment entailed and if there would be a spot to keep her K-9 close by.

As she and Everett walked down the hall toward the security office, their fingers brushed. She felt the impact shimmer all the way up her arm.

It had been difficult to concentrate after their brief but toe-curling kiss. One *she'd* initiated.

She had no idea what Everett thought of her doing such a thing; they'd been interrupted by Trent before they'd had a chance to discuss it.

Then, afterward, she'd felt foolish for thinking about his kiss when they were here to find Zoe. Her twin was her top priority. Deep down, she had a horrible feeling that Zoe's life wouldn't be worth much to the criminal ring after this last heist was finished.

The sense of urgency was impossible to ignore.

She and Everett were two of at least a dozen officers who reported for duty. After a quick rundown, they were sent to stand near the entrance of the grand ballroom.

At first, she felt conspicuous, as if everyone knew she and Everett didn't really belong. But, after several minutes, it was clear that none of the security members were chatting with each other. Their razor-like focus was clearly on the task at hand.

Guests were beginning to mingle, even though the hour was early and the party hadn't officially started. The room grew more crowded as the hour approached 7:00 p.m. Helena caught a glimpse of a striking man wearing a tuxedo, standing amid a group of people. She realized he was Jayson Porter, the billionaire owner of the hotel. The stunning woman at his side, dressed in a beautiful aquamarine floor-length gown, had an enormous teardrop diamond pendant hanging around her neck.

"Congratulations!" someone called, rushing toward the group.

Helena watched with bemusement as Jayson planted a kiss on the woman's lips. "Thank you.

I'm absolutely thrilled Camille has agreed to be my wife," he said in a loud, booming voice.

Many of the guests lifted glasses in a celebratory toast. Apparently, this was an engagement party, as well as a grand opening event. Did Cantwell and his boss know that?

Or was it just an added bonus?

The way the people were dressed, flashing more jewels than Helena had seen in her entire life, she figured it didn't matter.

Any one of them could be a target.

And where in the world was her sister? Helena's position was near one of the coffee stands. With the long skirt surrounding the table, it would make a good hiding place for Luna.

Catching Everett's gaze, she subtly gestured toward the table. He slowly nodded, giving his approval.

Helena didn't waste a second. She raced back to the suite, grabbed Luna by the leash and returned to the ballroom. She wasn't sure how she managed it, but soon the dog was lying beneath the skirted table without anyone noticing.

Breathing a sigh of relief, she caught a glimpse of a slender, auburn-haired woman wearing a server uniform enter the room carrying a tray.

Zoe wasn't a redhead but there was something about the way the woman moved that seemed—*familiar.* She found herself inching closer, trying to get a better look at her face.

The redhead turned just enough for Helena to see her full profile.

Zoe!

FIFTEEN

Helena's heart flooded with relief. Her sister was right there, on the other side of the room. As she began to nonchalantly make her way closer, Zoe set the tray down, turned and walked quickly back through the door from which she'd entered.

Was that a door leading to the kitchen? Had to be.

After a moment's hesitation, Helena changed course, taking a position near the wall so she could keep an eye on the doorway. As much as she wanted to rush in there to confront her sister, she didn't want to make a scene.

She touched her earpiece and checked the radio frequency was on channel eight. "Everett? I spotted Zoe. She's dressed as a server and has dyed her hair red."

"Good eye," Everett responded. "I haven't seen any sign of Cantwell yet, but I suspect he's close by. Try to get your sister off some-place alone."

"Ten-four." Sweeping her gaze around the room, Helena knew that wouldn't be easy. For one thing, more guests were arriving by the minute, each one dressed more glamorous than the next. Well, except for Camille—soon to be Mrs. Jayson Porter. Her aquamarine gown and flashy beauty made her a standout in the crowd.

Helena eased from her location near the side wall, trying not to catch anyone's attention. She didn't like not having Luna at her side but felt the need to remain as inconspicuous as possi-ble. She moved slowly, eyeing each of the serv-ers searching for her twin's familiar features.

Where in the world was Zoe?

This was the closest she'd been to her twin in well over a year. And she couldn't bear the thought of losing her again.

She had to convince Zoe to give herself up. She just had to!

Christine needed her mother. And Helena wanted her sister back, safe and sound.

"Did you see the size of the diamond around Camille's neck?" Everett asked, his voice low and husky in her ear. She suppressed a shiver. He was on the other side of the room, but her visceral reaction was as if he were standing right beside her.

"Yes." She raked her eyes across the room, trying to spot the beautiful woman who'd just gotten engaged to the billionaire owner. "Do you think that's the target?"

"Why not? The pendant and the new shiny diamond ring on her left hand would be worth more than all the loot they've stolen to date."

Everett's theory was chilling. Was it possible Zoe was the one assigned to steal that jewelry? The idea made her feel sick. "Okay, alert the entire security team and let's try to keep an eye on Camille. It won't be good for any of us if she gets hurt as a result of this."

"Ten-four."

Craning her neck, she was relieved to see the billionaire and his new fiancée were standing in the middle of a group of partygoers. At least the aquamarine dress was bright enough to spot in the crowd.

Helena continued to make her rounds discreetly through the ballroom. It had been nearly thirty minutes since she'd glimpsed Zoe and doubts began to creep in.

Had she imagined the similarities between the redhead and her sister? It was difficult to remain objective with her twin in the crosshairs.

One of the bartenders caught her eye and she frowned, thinking he looked familiar, too.

She watched him without seeming to, her mind whirling in an attempt to place him.

Then it hit her. *Cantwell.* Gareth Cantwell was dressed as a bartender.

She touched her earbud. "Everett, I see Cantwell behind the bar closest to you."

"Give me a minute to get a visual. Ten-four." There was nothing but silence as Helena scanned the room for Zoe. There were many servers coming and going, busy with bringing out trays of food, so it was difficult to keep track of each one.

Frustrated when there was no sign of the redhead, she turned on her earpiece again. "Everett? Do you see Cantwell or Zoe?"

"Negative." Everett was quiet for a heartbeat then asked, "Do you have eyes on Camille?"

A warning shiver snaked down her spine as she raked her gaze over the milling guests. The room was packed now, and music began to drift from strategically placed speakers, making it difficult to hear. "No. I don't see her, either."

"Let's make one more sweep then check the restrooms," Everett suggested.

"You stay in the ballroom. I'll head into the bathrooms." Helena knew from scoping the place out earlier that there were two sets of restrooms—one off each end of the ballroom. She paused to give Luna the hand signal to stay and then headed over to check the bathroom closest to her first. There were two pretty women at the counter refreshing their makeup. The white stall doors went all the way to the floor, so she couldn't look underneath them to check for the aquamarine dress.

After the two women left, she called out softly, "Ms. Camille?"

Nothing.

She tried every stall door, finding one locked. She knocked on the door. "I'm looking for Camille."

"Well she's not in here with me," a testy voice responded.

Feeling foolish, she responded, "My mistake. Sorry to bother you."

Helena returned to the main hallway that ran along the front of the ballroom. She tapped her ear buds to activate the two-way communication via the radio. "Nothing in the restroom to the right, heading to the other now."

"Got it, and be careful. I think Cantwell is on the move, I don't see him behind the bar anymore."

She didn't like the sound of that. As she turned the corner, she caught a glimpse of the redhead.

"Zoe!" Helena kept her voice low but urgent. "Zoe, wait."

The redhead turned to glance back. Zoe's eyes widened as she recognized Helena. Finally! She'd found her sister. Zoe had what appeared to be a velvet bag clutched in her hand. But, instead of stopping, her twin broke into a run.

"Zoe, don't go!" Helena went after her, but her sister disappeared behind another doorway. She reached up to activate her radio. "Everett, I'm following Zoe through a hallway parallel to the ballroom. Luna is still inside beneath the coffee table."

"Roger that."

It took precious seconds for Helena to catch up to her twin. She slammed through the door, surprised to find herself in a narrow hallway instead of the kitchen or food staging area.

Zoe must have sensed Helena behind her because she kept going, pushing through yet another door at the end of the narrow hall. Helena put on a burst of speed in an effort to catch up.

Suddenly she was outside and in the rear parking lot. Zoe's hands were now empty. Had her twin given the goods to someone else?

"Zoe," Helena snagged her sister's arm. "You need to come with me."

"No." Zoe yanked out of Helena's grip with a ferocity that surprised her. "Camille is in the restroom unconscious from being hit on the head. She needs help."

"You *attacked* her?" She couldn't hide her horror. "No, Zoe, please stop this madness right now. You have to turn yourself in, cut a deal with the police so we can reunite you with Christine."

"I won't go to jail, Helena. I won't!" Zoe spun away and broke into a run. Within seconds, her twin was swallowed by the trees and brush.

No. This wasn't supposed to end this way. Zoe was supposed to agree to turn herself in.

Instead, her twin had chosen to be a fugitive on the run.

Helena whirled around to run back inside. She needed Luna's help more than ever.

As much as she loved her twin, she couldn't let Zoe get away with assault and battery, not to mention grand theft.

There must be a way to change Zoe's mind about all this. There just had to be.

Everett ignored the chatter in his ear from the rest of the security team. First, he'd lost sight of Cantwell, who was actually shorter than he'd anticipated, with feet that did not look as if they fit into a size twelve hiking boot. And now he couldn't find Helena or Zoe.

Where was everyone?

He hated being out of the loop.

After changing his radio channel to the private one for just him and the two K-9 cops, he left the ballroom and headed down a narrow hallway. From the map of the property in his head, he sensed there was a kitchen that ran along the back of the ballroom, and from there likely to the parking lot located near the employee entrance.

What better way to escape?

As he burst through the first doorway, he nearly collided with Helena coming in. She looked frazzled, her eyes wide with alarm.

"Zoe ran into the woods! I'm getting Luna to track her scent."

"You want me to wait for you?" Everett asked.

"No. Call Will, so you can find the cave entrance he mentioned. I have a feeling that's where Zoe is headed. Also, let the rest of the security team know Camille is in the bathroom to the left of the ballroom and needs help. I believe Zoe hit her over the head and robbed her."

The news of Camille being harmed was disturbing. "Will do. And I'll get Will and Scout to join us at the cave."

"I'll be there ASAP." Helena ran past him, heading toward the ballroom.

It took every ounce of willpower he possessed to let her go alone. She was a trained state trooper and had a great partner in Luna.

Still, he didn't like it. Not one bit.

It occurred to him that he couldn't imagine what his life would be like without Helena. Would he see her again once this case was over?

Surprisingly, he wanted to. Very much.

As he continued to cross the asphalt parking lot, he touched his earpiece. After he let the hotel security team know to send a female guard into the restroom to find Camille, he called up Helena's team member on their own radio channel. "Will? You and Scout need to meet us in the cave behind the Grand Chalet. It's the likely hiding spot for Zoe and Cantwell, and whoever else is involved in this mess."

"Roger that, we're on our way."

Everett plowed into the woods, following the broken branches that he firmly believed had been left by Zoe and or Cantwell. Thankfully, the light sky helped him visualize the area without difficulty.

He couldn't believe Zoe had hit Camille over the head and robbed her, no doubt taking both the large diamond around her neck, as well as the new flashy engagement ring. Poor Helena. He'd have little choice but to arrest her twin once they finally caught up to her.

If only Zoe had stayed in his cabin with Christine. He and Helena could have kept them both safe.

Instead of now being forced to chase the young mother through Denali.

The woods grew thick, forcing him to slow his pace. The path was more difficult to follow now; there weren't nearly as many broken branches to indicate the path Zoe had taken.

He listened intently, trying to pinpoint the location of the cave. When he heard a dog bark, he smiled, thinking either Will and Scout had gotten there or Helena and Luna.

A border collie came bounding through the brush behind him. Glancing back over his shoulder, he spied Will Stryker not far behind.

"Where's Helena?" the trooper asked with a frown.

"She and Luna will be here soon." At least, Everett hoped so.

"We need to split up, come at the cave from different directions," Will said. "The cave entrance is roughly due east. I'll take Scout to the north, you take the south."

"Should we let Helena know?" Everett asked.

"I'll tried to raise her on the radio but didn't get a response."

Everett paled. "No response? That's not

very reassuring. She didn't have to go far to get Luna—the dog was in the ballroom."

"I wouldn't worry, she's probably just working with Luna in an effort to track Zoe." The other man didn't appear concerned.

Everett nodded and veered off toward the south, as Will had directed. Since the trooper had been in the cave before, and he hadn't, there was little choice but to follow his lead.

Still, he couldn't help glancing back over his shoulder, scanning the area for Helena.

The terrain began to climb and he caught a glimpse of an opening near some rocks. Not quite as large as the cave entrance he and Helena had found, but big enough for a man to enter walking upright.

He crouched behind a bush, keeping the cave entrance in sight. No one was near the opening. Nor could he see Will or Scout.

Touching his earpiece, he tried Helena. "Helena? Are you okay?"

No response. Did the wireless devices work this far out here in the woods? Maybe not.

But then he heard Will Stryker's voice in his ear. "Everett, I'm in position."

"Me, too," he responded.

"Let's approach, but cautiously," Will said.

"Roger that." Everett slowly rose and eased

toward the cave entrance, the hairs on the back of his neck lifting in alarm.

Helena's lack of response bothered him.

He lifted his heart in prayer. *Please God, keep Helena and Zoe safe in Your care.*

Helena had wasted precious seconds returning to the ballroom for Luna but had returned just in time to see Everett disappear into the woods.

The elkhound was hot on Zoe's trail, and Helena was thankful for her partner's ability to track people and apprehend suspects.

No doubt she'd need both of Luna's keen skills before this night was over.

The dog moved quickly through the brush, pursuing Zoe's scent. Helena had left Luna off leash, just in case they ran into Cantwell or one of the shooters. As she pushed through some thick brush, her earpiece fell out taking the small radio with it, but she didn't stop. She had her weapon in hand, but her palm was slick with sweat as she pushed leaves and branches out of the way to keep up with her K-9.

At one point, Luna doubled back to find her. She praised the dog then gave her the command. "Seek. Seek and get her!"

Luna whirled, her large tail wagging with excitement as she rushed back on Zoe's trail.

Helena thought she could see the cave entrance up ahead but had no idea where Will and Everett were. She hoped they hadn't gone into the cave without her providing backup.

Besides, once in the cave, there was no telling how deep Zoe had gone. Luna would be able to track her, but Scout's expertise was more around scenting narcotics.

Maybe Cantwell had drugs on him? She could only hope.

Helena felt someone come up behind her and turned, expecting to see Everett.

Only to find herself looking at the blunt end of a gun.

She froze, her gaze lifting to Cantwell's with a sinking feeling in her gut.

"Drop the gun." His voice was quietly intense. Every cop on the force knew you did whatever possible to avoid giving up your weapon, but she didn't see that she had much choice. The gun in Gareth Cantwell's hand was mere inches from her nose.

Impossible for her to disarm him.

Even calling Luna wouldn't work; he could just as easily shoot her partner. And no way was she allowing that to happen.

With painstaking slowness, she opened her fingers and dropped her weapon. It hit the soft earth without making a sound.

"Now what?" she asked, meeting his gaze defiantly. He might be armed, but she was still a trained state trooper.

And she wasn't going down without a fight.

"Get rid of the earpiece, too."

"I lost it already." She pointed at her ear, while her thoughts whirled. Had Luna already caught up with Zoe? She hoped and prayed the K-9 wouldn't come back to find her.

"Put your hands on your head and walk slowly into the cave," Cantwell ordered. "Do something stupid and I'll shoot you where you stand."

Once again, she complied. Turning her back on the man wasn't easy, and she mentally braced herself in case he decided to shoot her in the back.

Fortunately, he didn't.

"What do you want from me?" There must be some reason he was ordering her into the cave.

"I want the kid." Cantwell's statement was so shocking, she stumbled over a root and almost fell on her face.

"What? Why?" She glanced at him over her shoulder.

"It doesn't matter why, but I want that kid and you're going to get it for me."

It? Did he even know the baby's gender? "Because she's your daughter?"

"Shut up," Cantwell snapped.

Helena really didn't want to go into the cave with him, and furtively glanced around for either Will or Everett.

Someone had to be nearby and, once they saw what was happening, would back her up.

And what about Zoe? Where did her true loyalties lie?

Helena swallowed hard and stepped into the cool dimness of the cave.

Her mission was to stay alive long enough to escape.

SIXTEEN

Moving as quietly as possible, Everett made his way down one of the cave tunnels. But when he heard Gareth Cantwell's harsh voice telling Helena he wanted the kid and expected her to get *it* for him, he froze, his heart sinking to the soles of his feet.

Cantwell had Helena. But where was Luna? And Zoe?

"Call whoever has the kid, tell them to bring it here," Cantwell ordered. "Now!"

"The cop watching Christine doesn't know where this cave is located." Helena's voice was calm and rational. "You need to choose a better meeting point."

"I don't have to do anything," Cantwell snarled. "You have to get me that kid!"

"Okay, but again, it's not going to be easy for Trent to find this place. You could follow me to the suite, if you'd like."

"Oh, sure, like I'm going to walk into a trap

like that." Cantwell sounded as if he was losing his cool, which concerned Everett more than anything. Irrational men did unexpected things, like shooting first and asking questions later.

"Call the guy with the kid," he said. "And let him know if he tries to bring reinforcements, I'll kill you and anyone else who gets in my way."

Everett eased along the wall of the tunnel to get a visual of the main area of the cave. When he was close enough, he could see Helena standing, her hands laced on top of her head, with Cantwell holding his gun at her chest.

No weapon or radio, he noted. But he and Will were both in this cave, which gave them an advantage.

But first, he needed to draw the man's attention away from Helena.

Luna materialized next to him, her tall head brushing against his hand. Thankfully, he'd spent enough time with the K-9 that she saw him as a friend and not a foe.

Everett lowered to a crouch to put his arm around Luna's neck. "Easy, girl," he whispered.

The dog didn't move, as if sensing the danger Helena faced.

Now, about that diversion… His earpiece and small radio didn't weigh enough to make noise if he tossed it against the dirt wall. He needed a heavier object to get the job done.

But *what*?

He knelt and felt along the ground for something solid. After what seemed like forever, his fingers brushed against a rock about the size of an egg.

Rising, Everett eased forward, getting as close as possible to where Cantwell had Helena. He figured he'd toss the rock at the wall then tell Luna to get him, the command Helena had used.

And pray that nothing bad happened.

Before he could move, though, he heard a female voice. "Don't, Gareth. Leave Helena alone."

Zoe? Everett pressed his back against the wall, watching as Helena's twin emerged from the opening.

"I told you this sister of yours was a problem," Cantwell said in a snide voice.

"You don't need Helena or Christine. Take me instead." Zoe bravely faced Cantwell.

"I don't want you." There was a hint of disgust in Cantwell's tone. "You're of no use to me now. Haven't you caused enough trouble?"

"I got you Camille's diamonds, the way you told me to," Zoe shot back. "So don't act as if I haven't done my part in all of this. You promised Christine would be safe, but that was just another of your lies, wasn't it?"

"I never told you to get rid of the kid," Cantwell countered. "And that's a big problem."

Everett sensed they were at a stalemate. Zoe's presence complicated his plan. Big-time. He didn't want Cantwell to start shooting, possibly hitting Helena or Zoe.

He couldn't see any sign of Will and Scout, but imagined they were someplace nearby, likely closer to Zoe than he was. Everett sent up another quick prayer, asking for safety and guidance, then tossed the rock toward Cantwell.

"Get him!" Everett shouted.

Luna shot forward, growling low in her throat. At the same time, Helena dropped to the ground, sweeping her legs out to kick at Cantwell.

Cantwell fired his weapon, but his aim was high and wide as Luna grabbed hold of his ankle and yanked hard.

"Owwww," the man cried.

Helena lunged to her feet and grabbed his gun.

Meanwhile, Everett rushed into the large section of the cave, Stryker joining from the other tunnel.

In a heartbeat it was over.

Cantwell was down on the ground with Luna

growling in his face and Helena holding his gun on him.

"You're under arrest, Gareth Cantwell," Everett said, pulling a set of plastic zip ties from the pocket of his security uniform. "You have the right to remain silent, anything you say can and will be used against you in a court of law." He continued reciting the Miranda warning, as he tightened the zip ties around Cantwell's wrists.

"Luna, come." When she complied, Helena quickly praised her. "Good girl."

Everett had to admit that, without the K-9, this takedown could have ended very differently. "She's a great partner."

"Yes, she is. Zoe?" Helena called out without taking her gaze off Cantwell. "Are you okay?"

"Y-yes," her twin whispered. "But—I don't understand. Why does Gareth want Christine?"

Cantwell's mouth twisted into a sneer, but he didn't say a word, clearly taking his right to remain silent to heart.

"I don't know," Everett said, hauling Cantwell to his feet. "But we've known for a while that Christine was a target, and we checked the pink diaper bag and the infant seat from top to bottom, without finding a thing."

Cantwell's jaw dropped as if that was news to him. "Nothing?" he croaked.

"Why?" Everett eyed him blandly. "What were you expecting?"

Cantwell looked away. "I want a lawyer."

Of course he did. "You'll get one, once we have you booked, processed and safely stashed in jail." Everett hesitated then added, "If you're not in this alone, now is the time to tell us who else is involved."

Cantwell pursed his lips.

Everett knew the guy with the size twelve hiking shoe had to be out there somewhere. Or maybe he'd seen what was going down and taken off to avoid being caught.

They'd find out the truth. Hopefully sooner than later.

"A-am I under arrest, too?" Zoe's plaintive tone had Helena turning to face her twin.

"Yes, I'm afraid so," Helena said gently. "But if you cooperate with us, and give the diamonds back to Camille, we may be able to work with the DA to get you some sort of deal."

Zoe's eyes filled with tears. "I'm so sorry. I only did what Gareth wanted because he threatened to hurt my baby. Even after I dropped her off with Officer Brand, he kept telling me he knew exactly where Christine was and would hurt her."

"I understand," Helena said in a soothing voice. "But you should have come with me earlier, Zoe. That would have made it easier for us to cut a deal for you."

Zoe wiped at her eyes and sniffled loudly. "I know. I was just so panicked about the thought of going to jail—" Her voice broke.

"I'll do everything I can to get you the best lawyer possible," Helena promised.

Zoe sucked in a loud breath and nodded. "Okay. Gareth has the diamonds, and I can show you where the rest of his loot is hidden."

"That would definitely help your case," she told her sister. "Where is it?"

"Right here in the cave."

Everett, already in the process of running his hands down Cantwell's pant legs to make sure he didn't have a second gun, had momentarily forgotten about the theft. He patted Cantwell's pockets and found a soft velvet bag. Peering inside the bag, he aimed his light until he could see the large diamond pendant and the engagement ring.

"Both diamonds are here," he said. "That's good news and a step in the right direction, Zoe. The stolen goods being found on Cantwell makes it clear he's involved with the theft."

"I saw the area where Cantwell stashed his loot," Will interjected. "It's back that way." He jerked his thumb in the direction of the tunnel behind him.

"Let's check it out." Everett hesitated, realizing he couldn't leave Cantwell alone.

"Luna and I will keep an eye on him," Helena offered. "You know more about the stolen items than I do."

Everett glanced at her with admiration. It was all he could do not to haul her into his arms for a kiss. But he managed to restrain himself to offering a small nod. "Thanks, Helena. I won't be long."

"Take your time." She pinned Cantwell with a stern look. "He's not going anywhere. And if he tries to run, Luna will get him."

As if on cue, the K-9 growled, making Everett smile.

"Okay," Everett agreed, moving past Helena and Zoe to join Will.

The trooper and Scout headed further back into the tunnel. They went so far, he was beginning to feel a bit claustrophobic, until Will made another turn and gestured. "I was right about here when I realized Cantwell had Helena."

Everett nodded, using the flashlight app on his phone to better see what was inside.

Boxes lined the wall, full of electronic devices like phones and computers. Then there were two smaller metal boxes off to the side.

He opened the first one and found an impressive amount of cash tucked inside.

The second, larger box was full to the brim with jewelry. Everett whistled under his breath and poked through the precious stones, looking for the large diamond and sapphire taken from the anniversary party, along with the heavy gold chains.

There was no sign of those particular pieces, but there were plenty of other items in the box. More than enough.

Everett smiled with grim satisfaction. This would put Cantwell away for a long time.

Helena felt Zoe inch forward to stand beside her. "How is Camille? Will she be okay?"

Helena frowned. "I don't know. We sent the security team in to find her."

Her sister sucked in a harsh breath. "If she doesn't get better…"

"Try not to think the worst." Helena kept her gaze on Cantwell. "I'm sure Camille will be fine."

"I hope so," Zoe whispered.

Helena risked a glance at her twin. "And you really don't know why Cantwell wants Christine?"

Zoe shook her head.

"Is he Christine's father?" Helena asked.

"No," Cantwell barked bluntly.

Zoe didn't say anything for a long moment. "Yes. But I didn't tell him that. It was bad enough that he kept threatening to hurt the baby."

"What?" Cantwell looked outraged. "You never told me it was my kid."

"Stop it!" Zoe suddenly shouted. Even Luna was startled by the loud noise. "She's a baby, not an 'it.' And her name is Christine."

"Easy, Zoe," Helena cautioned. She didn't want her sister to lose control and start swinging at Cantwell. "He's going to prison, so it won't matter in the long run who the father is."

Zoe wiped at her eyes. "I've made so many mistakes," she mumbled.

Yeah, pretty much, Helena thought, but said, "You can move forward from here, Zoe. Co-operating with Everett is the first step toward being reunited with Christine."

"Okay." She sniffled loudly. "I…would like to see my baby. I missed her more than I thought possible."

"I'm sure you did." Helena was glad that Zoe's instincts as a mother were kicking in.

"We found his stash," Everett said, returning to the cave. "Let's call the park rangers, get them to pick up Cantwell for us."

"Sounds good. Let's go, Cantwell," Helena

directed. "And don't even think of running... Luna will easily chase you down like the animal you are."

Cantwell walked out of the cave, blinking at the brightness surrounding them.

Everett used his earpiece to alert the hotel's security team that they'd recovered the diamonds and needed the park rangers to assist in bringing in a prisoner.

As they retraced their steps to the hotel, Helena was relieved to find her gun where Cantwell had forced her to drop it. Further down the path, she also found her missing earpiece. She quickly inserted it so she could hear what was going on with the rest of the team.

By the time they reached the parking lot behind the hotel, several security members had gathered there, along with a bunch of park rangers, including Arch Hanley.

Helena kept a keen eye on Hanley, just in case he was involved with Cantwell and these thefts. But the guy quickly moved forward to take possession of the perp.

"Nice work, Helena and Everett," Arch said. "We have a temporary jail cell that has this guy's name on it. Just let me know when you need him transported to Anchorage."

"Will do," Everett agreed. "Thanks for your help."

Arch flashed a smile. "It's been our pleasure to work with some of Anchorage PD's finest."

Helena crossed over to the security manager, Ben Watterson. "How is Camille?"

Watterson raked her and Luna with a harsh gaze. "She's been taken to the closest hospital, but I'm not happy about any of this. You were supposed to help prevent anything from being stolen and no one was supposed to get hurt."

Helena swallowed hard and nodded. He had a right to be upset. "You're right, this didn't go as smoothly as I'd hoped."

Everett came up to stand beside her. "However, we have found the diamonds. Do you have a pair of gloves?" When Watterson nodded, he handed him the velvet bag. "And I heard through the radio chatter that Camille was awake and talking, so really, things could have been worse."

Watterson pulled on gloves, opened the velvet bag and removed the diamonds. "I'm sure Jayson and Camille will be glad to have these returned to them after using them as evidence, of course. The diamond alone is worth a quarter of a million dollars."

Helena tried not to gape. Who in their right mind wore something of that high a value around their neck?

As if reading her thoughts, Watterson continued. "I tried to convince Camille and Jayson not to flash their jewelry while at the party. To replace them with cubic zirconium just in case something like this happened, but they didn't listen."

"You suspected they'd be a target?" Helena asked.

Watterson grimaced. "Yeah, even before you and Brand came forward asking to be a part of the team." He glanced at Luna with frank curiosity.

"My K-9 partner was instrumental in bringing Cantwell down," she told him. "Despite the fact he was armed with a gun. As Everett said, this could have ended much worse."

"I guess you're right." Watterson heaved a heavy breath. "Unfortunately, the hotel manager and my boss isn't seeing it that way."

Helena understood the security manager's job was likely in jeopardy over recent events. Although it wasn't his fault Zoe had cornered Camille in the restroom. Or that Cantwell had threatened to harm Christine if her twin refused to follow through with the theft.

"They had a plan and we did our best to bring them to justice," she told Watterson. "That's all we can do, right?"

He shrugged, not convinced. Then he touched his earpiece. "Yes, sir, right away."

Watterson left the area, no doubt going to face the boss.

Helena was suddenly glad she worked as a K-9 state trooper, rather than in the private sector. Lorenza was a great leader and very fair. She made a mental note to connect with the colonel very soon.

"Helena?" Zoe's voice was timid. "Could I please see Christine? Just for a few minutes at least?"

Helena glanced at Everett, who gave a brief nod.

"Sure thing." Helena put her arm around her twin's shoulders. "I'll take you to see your baby now. She's in a suite with one of Everett's friends."

"I'll go with you," Everett offered. "I know I checked the diaper bag and infant seat very thoroughly, but maybe I missed something."

Will gestured back to the cave. "I don't feel good about leaving the stolen goods in there unprotected. Scout and I will stand guard until we can get the crime team out here."

Helena nodded in relief. "Thanks, Will, for everything."

"No problem." Her teammate glanced at Zoe, looked as if he might say something like *Why isn't she in handcuffs?* but turned and headed into the woods without voicing his thought.

Helena knew she should have placed Zoe under arrest already, but wanted to wait until after her twin had a chance to hold her baby.

Zoe deserved that much, didn't she?

With Zoe tucked between her and Everett, and Luna at her side, they headed into the hotel to where the suites were located.

Trent stood when they entered. "Everything okay?"

"Yeah, thanks." Everett clapped him on the back. "How was Christine?"

"She's a good kid, took her bottle like a champ," he said as Zoe rushed forward to lift Christine into her arms. "Am I officially off babysitting duty?"

"Yeah, I think we can take it from here," Everett told him. "We arrested Cantwell, and Will is standing guard over the stolen goods."

"Okay, I just got a message from our sergeant, he wants an update. I'll, uh, go outside to make the call, give you guys some privacy."

Trent left the suite, leaving the three of them and the baby alone.

A lump formed in the back of Helena's throat as she watched Zoe coo over Christine. The baby smiled up at her mother, as if recognizing her. It was heartwarming to watch them together, and only made Helena more determined to convince the DA to offer Zoe some sort of deal.

But the happy reunion was cut short when Luna began to growl low in her throat. Helena frowned. Now what?

The door to the suite opened, revealing a man she'd never seen before. He was holding a gun.

SEVENTEEN

"Give me that infant carrier and no one will get hurt."

Everett glanced from the plastic car seat in his hands to where his informant, Norbert Monroe, stood, pointing a gun at them.

What in the world? It didn't take but a moment to notice the size twelve hiking boots on Norbert's feet.

His blood turned to ice as he realized what a terrible mistake he'd made.

All this time, Norbert must have been tracking his phone, stringing him along under the pretense of providing key information on the robberies, while being here in Denali the entire time.

How had he made such a horrible error in judgment?

In a heartbeat, Everett was back in time, three years ago, when another gun had been used against his wife and son.

He'd lost his entire world in a split second. The kid's gun had gone off, and there'd been so much blood. Too much for him to stop it, although he'd tried. Dear Lord, how he'd tried.

Sheila and Colin had died in his arms.

Was he destined to make the same mistake here today?

No! Please, Lord, no. Not again.

"Didn't you hear me?" Norbert's voice rose as he waved the gun in frustration. "Hand me the carrier right now and no one will get hurt!"

Everett pushed the dark memories of the past away with a concerted effort. He had already looked at the infant seat once without finding anything, but clearly there was a reason the informant wanted it. He glanced at Helena and noticed she seemed just as confused.

From the corner of his eye, he noticed Zoe turning away from Norbert, shielding Christine with her body as she sank behind the meager protection of a chair. Every mother's instinct was to protect her child. That was exactly what Sheila would have done.

He could also tell that Luna's continued growling was getting on the man's nerves, and that was concerning. Everett knew only too well how a tenuous situation like this could spiral out of control.

"Okay, that's fine, Norbert." He kept his tone

calm. "You can have it. Just point the gun at the floor, okay? I can't give you anything until I'm sure you won't shoot at us."

"No. Give me the carrier *right now*!" Norbert was looking less and less stable, his eyes darting back and forth across the room.

The guy was likely high on drugs, which was even more worrisome. Just like the kid who'd killed his family.

Everett caught a glimpse of Helena giving Luna a subtle hand signal. He recognized the command. As the dog leaped forward, he threw the empty infant carrier at Norbert with all his might.

The dog clamped her teeth around his ankle. Norbert howled in pain and tried to aim the nose of the gun at the K-9 just as the infant carrier sailed toward him. Norbert instinctively lifted his hands, as if to catch it, at the same moment Luna pulled him off balance.

The infant carrier slammed into him then bounced away, hitting the floor with a loud crash. Norbert lost his grip on the gun as he fell on his back within arm's length of the carrier. Still howling in pain, he tried to crawl toward the infant seat, but Everett was on him.

"No-o!" Norbert didn't give up without a fight. He swung a fist but Everett easily ducked and grabbed his wrist in a tight grip.

"Get him," Helena commanded.

Luna grabbed his ankle with her mouth, tightening until he cried out once again. "She's biting me! Get that dog off me!"

"You're under arrest," Everett said, gripping Norbert's wrists tightly to prevent him from taking another cheap shot. "For attempting to shoot a police officer."

"I didn't," Norbert whined.

"You did," Helena spoke up. "Luna, heel." The K-9 backed off but didn't go too far.

Everett wrenched the man's arm up and flipped him onto his stomach. Using the plastic ties in his security uniform pocket, he quickly bound his wrists together, all the while reciting the Miranda warning. Helena came over to help him haul Norbert into a sitting position so they could also bind his ankles.

Norbert Monroe wasn't going anywhere except directly to lockup.

"That was too close," Zoe whispered, straightening from her pseudo hiding place and running a gentle hand over her daughter's head.

"I know," Helena agreed softly, crossing to hug her twin. Luna followed, wagging her tail as if in agreement. "I think you're finally safe now, Zoe. Christine, too."

"Thanks, Helena." Zoe's tone was contrite.

"I was so stupid, wasn't I? I should have come to you for help a long time ago."

"Yes, but like I said, you need to move forward from here, Zoe. Concentrate on making good decisions from this moment forward," Helena reminded her. "And that means cooperating with the DA's office and testifying against both Norbert and Cantwell."

"I will," Zoe promised.

The twin's reunion was touching, but Everett had questions that needed answers. "How did you track me here in Denali National Park?" Everett crouched on his haunches to peer into his former informant's face. "I never would have pegged you to be a phone tracing expert."

Despite being cuffed and under arrest, Norbert preened. "My sister's son is one of those techno geeks," he boasted. "Sean figured out how to do it and kept me up to date with every call you made. Pretty good, huh? For a cop, you're not that smart. You never suspected me, did you?"

"No, I didn't," Everett responded honestly. And that was a mistake that would haunt him for a long time. "Why did you want the infant carrier anyway?"

Norbert clamped his mouth shut and looked away, as if finally deciding cooperation wasn't in his best interest.

Everett stared at him for several long moments in an effort to wait him out, but Norbert didn't cave.

Turning, he rose and went over to retrieve the infant seat from where it had fallen to the ground after bouncing off Norbert. He picked it up and once again checked the plastic cushion for any signs of tampering.

But, as before, he found nothing.

He flipped it over, examining the underside. Beneath the straps used to secure the baby, he noticed a significant crack in the plastic, likely from when it hit the floor. Prying his fingertips into the narrow opening, he was able to pull a slight square section away, revealing a small space stuffed with some sort of cloth.

His pulse jumped with anticipation. "Well, what do we have here?" Everett glanced at Helena as he pulled the cloth bag from the hiding spot. Unfolding the cloth, a large diamond and several heavy gold chains fell into the palm of his hand.

The same items Norbert had claimed he'd witnessed Zoe handing over to some guy he didn't know.

"That's where the diamond and gold chains went?" Zoe echoed incredulously. "I don't understand. All this time, the diamond and chains were tucked in Christine's car seat?"

"Apparently so," Everett said, drilling Norbert with a narrow look. "Seems as if my informant must have stolen the goods from Cantwell, then hid them in what he thought might be a safe spot."

Zoe spun toward Norbert. "Not directly from Cantwell, but from me. You *louse*! You were the one who was there that day Gareth and I had the big fight over the missing diamond and gold chains. Gareth accused me of stealing them for myself, when it was *you*. You stole from Gareth and blamed me."

Norbert grimaced but remained silent.

"And all this time, they were in Christine's infant carrier." Zoe shook her head in disgust. "You put an innocent child in danger over stolen jewelry."

Again, Norbert didn't respond.

"Cantwell must have suspected one of you hid the items in something connected to Christine," Helena said. "That's why he asked for the kid. Either to find what you stole, or to use her as leverage against Zoe to find the missing jewelry."

Zoe rubbed her temple. "I guess it's a good thing I dropped the baby at Everett's cabin."

"Yeah." Everett tossed the cloth aside, when another small device fell out. He quirked a brow, holding up the USB drive for Helena to see.

"Wonder what information we'll find on this?" He glanced at Norbert, hoping the guy would give up the details.

"I—I'm pretty sure that's a record of everything Gareth stole," Zoe admitted. "He was determined to reach a specific dollar amount before he relocated to the Lower 48 to dispose of the stolen goods." Then she grimaced. "At least, up until this most recent job at the Denali Grand Chalet, which was supposed to be the last haul before leaving Alaska for good."

Everett turned the USB drive over in his hand, thinking about the stash in the cave. "So everything in the cave is itemized on this drive?"

Zoe clutched Christine close and nodded. "As far as I know, yes."

"Very helpful," Everett said. He tucked the USB drive in with the diamond and gold chains. How great to have a nicely organized list of everything Cantwell had stolen to match up to the goods they'd located in the cave.

It was finally over.

No thanks to him.

Assailed by guilt over how he'd trusted Norbert, Everett knew in that moment he didn't deserve a second chance.

Helena, Zoe and the most innocent of all,

baby Christine, had almost died today because of him. Because he'd trusted the wrong guy.

Maybe it was time to rethink his career as a cop.

How many mistakes like this before he caused someone else to be killed? His gaze lingered for a moment on Helena.

He had nothing to offer her except a shell of the man he'd once been.

Helena eyed her sister, wondering if Zoe really hadn't known about the jewelry stashed in Christine's infant carrier.

Her twin had looked and sounded surprised, but it was difficult to fully trust what she was telling her.

She glanced at Everett, who appeared lost in thought. She moved toward him. "What do you think?" she asked in a low voice.

He blinked. "About what?"

She waved at her twin, who held Christine as if she might never let the baby go. "Do you believe her?"

"I don't know what to believe anymore." His voice was low and ragged. "I've made so many mistakes…"

"What are you talking about?"

"Nothing." Everett took a step back and

pulled out his phone. From outside the suite, they could hear ringing.

Helena realized Trent must be outside somewhere. Her blood ran cold as she realized Norbert must have used Trent's key to access the hotel suite.

Everett's brain had been one step ahead of hers, because he was already barreling out the door. Helena glanced at Luna. "Guard," she commanded.

Luna immediately went over to sit straight and tall right in front of Norbert.

Satisfied their prisoner wasn't going anywhere, she joined Everett outside, where he had the door to the black SUV open and was reaching in to check on Trent.

The officer's phone was lying on the ground, near the front tire, where it must have dropped during the struggle.

"Trent? Are you okay?"

The officer who was draped over the steering wheel, where he must have been knocked out, let out a low groan. Trent lifted his head, opened his eyes and put a hand to his head. "I'm sorry, Everett. I never should have let him get the drop on me."

"It's not your fault," Everett said in a low voice. "But we need to get you to the closest hospital."

"Nah, I'm okay." Trent grimaced as he shifted in the SUV. "What about the baby? Is she hurt?"

"Christine is fine," Helena assured him. "I'll get you an ice pack for your head." She smiled grimly. "I know from personal experience that ice helps diminish the throbbing pain."

"Come inside the suite," Everett added. "I'll call the park rangers back to take Norbert to jail. He'll enjoy being locked up with Cantwell."

And what about Zoe? Helena didn't voice her concern but knew that based on her twin's assault and robbery of Camille, she should be in handcuffs, too, and taken to jail along with Everett's informant.

As much as it pained her to turn in her sister, Helena knew it was the right thing to do.

Inside the suite, Zoe had taken a seat on one of the chairs, still gazing down at her daughter. Helena swallowed against a hard lump of emotion and went into the kitchenette to get ice from the mini freezer. Balling the cubes into a cloth, she handed it to Trent, who'd dropped into a chair across from Zoe.

"Thanks," he said, lifting the makeshift cold pack to the bump on the back of his head. He sighed. "You're right, that does feel better."

Norbert smirked from his spot on the floor.

But the expression of smug satisfaction faded as Luna leaned in, breathing into his face.

"Call the dog off," Norbert whined.

Helena ignored him, turning to Everett. His stricken expression seared her heart. "Hey, he'll be okay."

Everett gave a short shake of his head. "My fault," he said in a harsh tone. "It's all my fault."

It wasn't and, somewhere deep inside, Everett knew it, but he was allowing his emotions to cloud his judgment. And she understood where he was coming from.

Norbert Monroe had been his informant, the trusted source of inside information. Instead, he'd been tracking them through the Denali mountains.

But it wasn't as if they hadn't had other suspects, as well. Including Cantwell, Park Ranger Hanley and her sister.

That brought her back to Zoe.

"Did you call the park rangers yet?" she asked, changing the subject.

In answer, Everett pulled out his phone. She reached over and put her hand on his arm to prevent him from making the call. In a soft voice, she said, "Wait, first we need to talk about Zoe."

"What about her?" Everett glanced over to

where Zoe was in the kitchen making a bottle for Christine, who'd begun to fuss.

"We need to place her under arrest for assault and grand theft," Helena pointed out.

Everett slowly nodded. "I know. I was thinking we'd take her back to Anchorage with us, to turn her in there. That way, we can talk to the DA right away, to cut a deal in exchange for her cooperation. I don't want her stuck in jail with Cantwell and Norbert."

"Really?" Helena was touched by his offer. "I...don't know what to say."

He shrugged, his gaze skating from hers in a way that made her frown. "It's nothing. I know that Zoe is complicit in this to a certain extent, but Cantwell held her baby's life over her head. That has to count toward extenuating circumstances."

"Oh, Everett. Thank you." Helena stepped forward to embrace him, but he hastily moved back to avoid her, as if she were contaminated with some highly contagious disease.

"Don't thank me," he said harshly.

"Everett, what's going on?" She stared at him, feeling helpless in the face of his anger.

"Nothing." He turned away and lifted his phone. "Arch? It's Brand. We have another of Cantwell's accomplices here at the Grand Chalet. Would you mind sending someone out to pick him up? He belongs in jail with Cantwell. Oh, and we need a ranger to relieve K-9 Trooper Will Stryker in the cave where we found the stolen goods."

Helena couldn't hear the ranger's side of the conversation, but Everett nodded as he listened.

"Good, see you in five minutes." He gave the suite number and glanced at Norbert. "You're going away for a long time, Monroe. Assaulting a police officer, for starters, and adding the thefts and attempted shooting of another police officer means you won't see the light of day for years to come."

Monroe's lips thinned but he didn't respond. Maybe because Luna hadn't moved from her position since Helena had ordered the K-9 to guard him.

The park rangers arrived and quickly took custody of Norbert Monroe. Everett walked out with them, likely giving them the details of why the guy had been arrested.

Helena, troubled by Everett's withdrawal, was hoping for an opportunity to talk to him alone. She turned to Zoe. "When you're finished feeding Christine, make sure the car seat is still safe to use. It's too late tonight, but we'll need to head back to Anchorage first thing in the morning."

"Okay." To her credit, Zoe didn't complain.

The way she stared down at her baby made Helena's heart swell with hope.

"I'll watch Christine while you work with the DA's office," she added.

"I know you will." Zoe smiled. "You're going to be a wonderful aunt."

She couldn't wait. Glancing at her watch, she frowned. Where was Everett? She headed outside to look for him.

What she found was a note tucked beneath the wiper blade of Trent's SUV. Battling a wave of apprehension, she pulled the note out and unfolded it.

Helena, please drive Trent back to Anchorage with Zoe and Christine in the morning. I'll find my own way back. E.

A deep chill seeped into her bones as she realized her time with Everett was over.

He was gone. As if they'd never worked together in tracking Zoe. Had never hugged or kissed. Had never bonded over caring for Christine.

It was over.

EIGHTEEN

Everett hitched a ride with the park rangers back to his first rental cabin. It's where he'd left his personal SUV in what seemed like eons ago. On the drive, he'd learned the park rangers had released Will Stryker from guard duty and were in the process of preserving the evidence of Cantwell's stash from the cave with the help of forensic scientist, Tala Ekho, who'd been flown into Denali by bush plane.

Scrubbing his hands over his face, he tried not to imagine how Helena would react when she read his hastily scrawled note. He should have taken more time with choosing his words, so it wouldn't feel like a slap in the face after the way she'd tried to embrace him.

He was still shocked at how Helena had attempted to hug him.

As if he hadn't almost gotten her killed. Not to mention placing Zoe and Christine in danger, too.

Helena was better off without him. She was a believer and...well, despite how he'd fallen back into the habit of praying, still didn't understand how God could love him while taking his young wife and son away forever.

Yet the sixteen-year-old who'd stolen their lives had survived to live out a good portion of his life in jail.

Why? Why was that part of some grand plan?

As always, he couldn't make any sense of it.

From nowhere, a long-forgotten Bible verse flashed in his mind.

In Him we have redemption through His blood, the forgiveness of sins, according to the riches of His grace which He made to abound toward us in all wisdom and prudence, having made known to us the mystery of His will, according to His good pleasure which He purposed in Himself, that in the dispensation of the fullness of the times He might gather together in one all things in Christ.

A wave of shame washed over him. Hadn't God sent Jesus to save them? Sacrificing his son, to forgive their sins? As Helena had pointed out, who was he to question God's will? Losing his wife and son had been heartbreaking, but Helena was right to remind him that he was here today for a reason.

For a second chance?

No. He instinctively veered away from that thought.

Standing in the center of the cabin they'd left in such a hurry just a handful of days ago, he noticed everything looked the same yet also different. Not just because of Helena's state trooper hat lying on the floor partially hidden behind the sofa, but almost as if he were seeing the place with new eyes.

As an older and wiser man? Maybe.

Crossing over, he picked up her hat, smoothing his hand over the wide flat brim. Helena was completely different from Sheila, mostly because she was a cop, just like he was. A cop trained to serve and protect the citizens of Alaska.

The way he'd put her in danger was unacceptable. Yet she'd also held her own, using her K-9 partner to the animal's fullest potential.

Was that the reason he couldn't get her out of his mind?

Glancing out the window, he noticed the sun had disappeared behind the mountain, bringing darkness.

Midnight.

He raked his hand over his head and decided to spend the night here before hitting the road.

No point in reaching Anchorage at four in the morning.

Despite his bone-weary exhaustion, Everett didn't sleep well. Memories of his time spent with Helena and Christine kept looping through his head like a movie reel. Helping Helena navigate caring for a three-month-old baby, sharing chores and meals together.

The way he'd felt like a part of her family kept nagging at him.

He didn't want or deserve a family.

Did he?

The following morning, Everett cleaned out the cabin and packed his things in his SUV. He set Helena's hat on the passenger seat.

He'd told himself he'd only see her again to return the hat, not for any other reason. Certainly not because he desperately wanted to share something other than a case with her.

His SUV ate up the miles between Denali and Anchorage, the tourist traffic unusually light for this time of the year. He'd occasionally glance at the hat, thinking about how to go about giving it back to her.

When he finally arrived in Anchorage, he realized he didn't know where Helena lived. Should he call her? Or contact Will Stryker to see if he'd be willing to tell him where she might be?

Rather than head home, Everett drove to the Anchorage police precinct, knowing it was well past time to update his boss about how things had transpired in Denali. Not to mention, he'd have a mile of paperwork to complete. Like most cops, he hated paperwork, but it was necessary to document all aspects of the case so no slick defense lawyer Cantwell and Monroe tried to hire could poke holes in what they'd done.

He entered the building, gave a nod to the desk clerk and then headed toward the back offices. Upon passing the interview rooms, he caught a glimpse of Helena holding Christine on her lap, Luna sitting tall at her side, while Zoe was talking to one of his fellow officers and some guy dressed in a suit. Likely the DA.

Helena pressed a kiss to the top of Christine's head. His heart squeezed and he stumbled to an abrupt stop.

A wave of emotion washed over him, nearly bringing him to his knees.

He loved her.

The realization was astounding. How was it possible that he'd fallen in love with Helena Maddox? He tried to force the image of Sheila and Colin into his mind, but it didn't work. Instead his gaze was riveted on Helena, her furry K-9 and Christine.

And the possibility of a future. One he'd never dared allow himself to imagine.

As if sensing his intense scrutiny, Helena turned and captured his gaze. A flash of wounded uncertainty crossed her features.

An avalanche of guilt pummeled him.

What had he done? He'd never intended to hurt her. Without hesitation, he crossed over and opened the door to the interview room. Luna wagged her tail in greeting. Officer Crowe and DA Blackwell looked up in surprise, but Everett didn't acknowledge either of them.

"Helena, could I speak to you in private for a moment?"

The way she hesitated made him wonder if she was going to tell him to take a hike, but she handed Christine over to Zoe and murmured, "I'll be back soon."

She stood and moved forward, Luna at her side. He held the door for them, gesturing to the main entrance leading outside. She wordlessly followed him into the bright sunshine.

Luna walked all the way to the end of her leash, sniffing the grass with canine curiosity.

"What do you want from me, Everett?" Helena lifted her chin and looked him directly in the eye. "You made your feelings perfectly clear."

That was news to him, since his feelings

were nothing but a jumbled mess in his mind. "I'm sorry. I never should have left without talking to you."

She lifted a slim shoulder and glanced over to where Luna was still exploring. "There's really no need to apologize. We wrapped up the case, right? That ended our time together."

He flinched at the blunt statement. "I'm apologizing for running away from my feelings. Do you realize how I nearly got you, Christine and Zoe killed in Denali? Not just once, but twice? Norbert was *my* informant. If I hadn't called him, we never would have been tracked down from safe house to safe house."

"Everett, you know as well as I do that cops aren't perfect. We make mistakes. We trust people we shouldn't. I've done the same thing." She stared at him, for a long moment. "Think about this case. How I chose to believe Zoe wasn't really involved in the thefts, only to have her confess about hitting Camille over the head and stealing her jewelry. You can't get any more culpable than that."

He shook his head. "It's not the same thing. Zoe is your twin sister. Of course you wanted to believe in her innocence. Norbert Monroe was a petty criminal turned informant. I never, ever, should have trusted him."

"Cops use informants all the time," she countered. "Sometimes they work out well, providing us inside information we wouldn't have gotten any other way. Other times, not so much. Maybe you should cut yourself a little slack, Everett. You had no way of knowing Norbert had worked with and, frankly, double-crossed Cantwell. My sister is the one who got involved in the criminal ring in the first place. Does that mean I'm responsible for her poor decisions?"

"Of course not." The denial was swift and he belatedly realized she had a point. He wasn't completely responsible for Norbert's decisions.

Cantwell's, either.

But he had to acknowledge his own actions. Like the way he'd tried to talk that sixteen-year-old into giving up his gun. At the time, he'd berated himself for doing something so foolish, but deep down, he was forced to admit he'd done exactly what he'd been trained to do.

Training that was ingrained in every cell of his body since joining the police academy ten years ago.

Maybe, just maybe, he wasn't entirely responsible for Sheila and Colin's deaths. The fault rested on the drug-induced haze of a young teenager's mind.

And if he'd have killed that kid? Would it not have been just as difficult to live with himself after something like that?

Yes. It would. The tightness in his chest loosened as he let go of the remaining vestiges of guilt.

His future was the beautiful, smart and talented woman standing right in front of him. If he was courageous enough to reach out and take it.

Helena was glad Everett had come to talk to her, but watching the myriad emotions flash over his features made her realize he still wasn't ready to let go of the past.

And she could understand how difficult it must be, considering how he'd lost his wife and son in the blink of an eye.

She never should have allowed Everett to wiggle his way into her heart. There was no one to blame but herself.

Somehow, she'd find a way to get over him.

She tugged on Luna's leash, bringing the dog to her side. Resting her hand on her K-9 partner's head, she decided honesty was the best approach.

"Everett, what happened that day you lost your wife and son was terribly tragic. I can only imagine how much you miss them. But try to remember God is always watching over us." Her smile slid sideways. "I care about you, Everett, very much. In fact, I've fallen in love with you, only I know it's too soon. That this isn't something you're ready for, and truly, I understand. My hope is that someday you'll find a way to let go of what you've lost and embrace the possibility of falling in love in the future."

Everett smiled and took a step closer. "I was hoping you'd say that."

She gaped, wondering if she'd missed something. "Say what?"

His smile widened. "There's more than just the possibility of me falling in love. It's already happened, Helena. I'm glad to hear you love me, because the feeling is mutual. I love you, too."

She eyed him doubtfully. What could have changed from his leaving the note last night and showing up here at the precinct this morning? "Are you sure you're not mistaking care and friendship for love?"

"I'm absolutely sure I love you," he repeated, his brown gaze clinging to hers. "And I'm happy to repeat it over and over until you believe me."

She wanted to. Oh *how* she wanted to believe him. Still, she hesitated. "What about—having a family? After spending time with Christine, I've realized how much I want to have a baby of my own someday."

"I would love to have a child with you, Helena," he said with a sweet smile. "But I think you should probably marry me first."

She flushed, wondering if she'd lost her mind to say such a thing. But Everett dropped to one knee and took her hand in his. Luna came over to nudge him, wanting to play, so he looped one arm around the Norwegian elkhound's neck, drawing Luna close while keeping his gaze on Helena's.

"Helena and Luna, will you please do the honor of marrying me? I'm sorry I don't have a ring to place on your finger, but I can offer my heart. I love you and don't want to live without you and your K-9 by my side."

"Oh, Everett." Tears pricked her eyes. "Yes, of course I'll marry you, and Luna already adores you, too."

"I'm glad." He stood and swept her into his arms, the way she'd longed for since they'd shared their first kiss.

This kiss was even sweeter, laced with the hope and promise of a beautiful future together.

"I love you, Everett," she whispered when she could breathe.

Luna pressed close, as if wanting to be a part of their embrace.

"I love you, too," he responded in a low, husky voice. He reached down to stroke Luna's fur. "I especially love that you're a package deal. Luna is amazing and did her part in keeping us all safe."

That made her laugh. "Don't forget my package deal includes Zoe and Christine."

He smiled again and, for the first time, she noticed the shadows of his troubled past had vanished from his eyes. "I'm counting on it. We can practice caring for Christine until we have a baby of our own."

"Practice, huh?"

She glanced back at the precinct where her twin was inside providing information to Officer Crowe and DA Blackwell. "Sounds like Zoe won't have to do much jail time, less than six months, so what do you think about a Christmas wedding?" She hesitated before adding, "A church wedding?"

"Christmas is a long way off," he protested, a teasing glint in his eye. "But if that's what you want, I'm happy to oblige, church wedding and all."

She went up on her tiptoes to kiss him again then rubbed her hand over Luna's fur. "Should we head back inside?"

"Of course." He slid his arm around her waist. "Oh, and by the way, I have your state trooper hat in my car."

She looked up at him in surprise. "Really? You brought it back for me?"

"Well, actually, I was going to hold it hostage until you agreed to marry me." He pressed a kiss to her temple. "I guess this means you can have it back."

She laughed, her heart filled with hope, love and happiness. She sent up a silent prayer of gratitude.

Thank you, God, for bringing Everett into my life!

* * * * *

*Look for the next book in the
Alaska K-9 Unit series,* Deadly Cargo
by Jodie Bailey.

*Alaska K-9 Unit
These state troopers fight for justice with the
help of their brave canine partners.*

Alaskan Rescue *by Terri Reed*
Wilderness Defender *by Maggie K. Black*
Undercover Mission *by Sharon Dunn*
Tracking Stolen Secrets *by Laura Scott*
Deadly Cargo *by Jodie Bailey*
Arctic Witness *by Heather Woodhaven*
Yukon Justice *by Dana Mentink*
Blizzard Showdown *by Shirlee McCoy*
Christmas K-9 Protectors
by Lenora Worth and Maggie K. Black

Dear Reader,

I hope you are enjoying *Tracking Stolen Secrets*, the fourth book in the Alaska K-9 Unit series. This has been a fun one to write with lots of new dog breeds along with adding the wilderness aspect.

As always, this series wouldn't be possible if not for our fabulous editor, Emily Rodmell, and a very talented team of authors. I'm blessed to be included as one of them.

I adore hearing from my readers!

I can be found through my website at https://www.laurascottbooks.com, via Facebook at https://www.facebook.com/LauraScottBooks, and Twitter https://twitter.com/laurascottbooks. Also, take a moment to sign up for my monthly newsletter. All subscribers receive a free novella, *Starting Over*, which is not available for purchase on any platform.

Until next time,
Laura Scott

Get 4 FREE REWARDS!

We'll send you 2 FREE Books plus 2 FREE Mystery Gifts.

Harlequin Heartwarming Larger-Print books will connect you to uplifting stories where the bonds of friendship, family and community unite.

FREE Value Over $20

YES! Please send me 2 FREE Harlequin Heartwarming Larger-Print novels and my 2 FREE mystery gifts (gifts worth about $10 retail). After receiving them, if I don't wish to receive any more books, I can return the shipping statement marked "cancel." If I don't cancel, I will receive 4 brand-new larger-print novels every month and be billed just $5.74 per book in the U.S. or $6.24 per book in Canada. That's a savings of at least 21% off the cover price. It's quite a bargain! Shipping and handling is just 50¢ per book in the U.S. and $1.25 per book in Canada.* I understand that accepting the 2 free books and gifts places me under no obligation to buy anything. I can always return a shipment and cancel at any time. The free books and gifts are mine to keep no matter what I decide.

161/361 HDN GNPZ

Name (please print)

Address   Apt. #

City   State/Province   Zip/Postal Code

Email: Please check this box ☐ if you would like to receive newsletters and promotional emails from Harlequin Enterprises ULC and its affiliates. You can unsubscribe anytime.

Mail to the **Harlequin Reader Service:**
IN U.S.A.: P.O. Box 1341, Buffalo, NY 14240-8531
IN CANADA: P.O. Box 603, Fort Erie, Ontario L2A 5X3

Want to try 2 free books from another series! Call 1-800-873-8635 or visit www.ReaderService.com.

HARLEQUIN SELECTS COLLECTION

19 FREE BOOKS IN ALL!

From Robyn Carr to RaeAnne Thayne to Linda Lael Miller and Sherryl Woods we promise (actually, GUARANTEE!) each author in the Harlequin Selects collection has seen their name on the *New York Times* or *USA TODAY* bestseller lists!

YES! Please send me the **Harlequin Selects Collection**. This collection begins with 3 FREE books and 2 FREE gifts in the first shipment. Along with my 3 free books, I'll also get 4 more books from the Harlequin Selects Collection, which I may either return and owe nothing or keep for the low price of $24.14 U.S./$28.82 CAN. each plus $2.99 U.S./$7.49 CAN. for shipping and handling per shipment*.If I decide to continue, I will get 6 or 7 more books (about once a month for 7 months) but will only need to pay for 4. That means 2 or 3 books in every shipment will be FREE! If I decide to keep the entire collection, I'll have paid for only 32 books because 19 were FREE! I understand that accepting the 3 free books and gifts places me under no obligation to buy anything. I can always return a shipment and cancel at any time. My free books and gifts are mine to keep no matter what I decide.

☐ 262 HCN 5576   ☐ 462 HCN 5576

Name (please print)

Address   Apt. #

City   State/Province   Zip/Postal Code

Mail to the **Harlequin Reader Service:**
IN U.S.A.: P.O. Box 1341, Buffalo, NY 14240-8531
IN CANADA: P.O. Box 603, Fort Erie, Ontario L2A 5X3